MW01141827

"Carmen tak on an adventure of survival, culture, assimilated beliefs and horsemanship. Her characters exhibit strong will, strong beliefs, and hearts of courage. Readers will be delighted with each and every page turned. Pure enjoyment."

–Luanne Finley, Colville Tribal Descendant;
Lifetime Reservation Rancher

"Carmen Peone loves young people and horses. Heart of Courage is a genuine story of a Native American teen's struggle to honor her heritage as she reaches for the dreams that God has put in her heart. Rich in culture and backdrop, the narrative is warm, engaging, and indeed breathtaking at times. If you love kids and horses, you will love this book!"

–Sue Jacobsen,
4-H Leader for 18 years

"A very moving and fast-paced story of young Spupaleena, who tries to fulfill her own dreams and aspirations while trying to gain the approval and shed the disapproval of her father. Through Spupaleena, author Carmen Peone has incorporated her own Love of God, Love of horses, and desire to fulfill her own dreams of life."

–Rosalie J. Heath,
Retired Elementary Teacher

Heart
of
Courage

Heart
of
Courage

Carmen Peone

TATE PUBLISHING
AND **ENTERPRISES**, LLC

Published by Tate Publishing & Enterprises, LLC
127 E. Trade Center Terrace | Mustang, Oklahoma 73064 USA
1.888.361.9473 | www.tatepublishing.com

Tate Publishing is committed to excellence in the publishing industry. The company reflects the philosophy established by the founders, based on Psalm 68:11,
"The Lord gave the word and great was the company of those who published it."

Book design copyright © 2012 by Tate Publishing, LLC. All rights reserved.
Cover design by Shawn Collins
Interior design by Joel Uber

Published in the United States of America
ISBN: 978-1-61777-910-7
1. Fiction; Fantasy, Historical
2. Social Science; Customs & Traditions
12.01.13

Dedication

To my husband and best friend, Joe,
you are the rock I lean on.

Acknowledgements

*Thank you to Loren Marchand, three-time win-
ner of the Omak Stampede Suicide Race and winner
of multiple Native American track and relay races,
for sharing your experiences with me. Your expertise
and amazing ability to jockey are truly inspiring.
You are the "King of the Hill".*

Arrow Lakes Language Sound Guide

The <u>K</u> is a guttural K sound which is used deep in the throat.

The "<u>who</u>" is a soft blowing sound, not the word who.

The <u>huh</u> is a sound that comes from the back of the throat, as if one has something stuck in the back of the throat and is trying to get it out.

The <u>lth</u> sound is a lisping sound when the tongue is placed behind the front teeth and one blows softly.

The <u>ch</u> sound is a sharp ch not a soft ch sound.

The "K" with no bar is a soft k sound.

Note: The names used in this book are traditional animal names given to the people of the Arrow Lakes Tribe.

Chapter 1

"Never in this life will you ever be able to race your skinny, little pony with the men in our village!" ***Hahoola<u>who</u>*** ("Rattlesnake") laughed and then spit on the dirt in front of ***Spupaleena's*** ("Rabbit's") moccasins. Tangled, black hair ran down the length of his sweat soaked back as he sat on his horse, glaring down at the girl.

Spupaleena, seventeen-years-old and completely determined, narrowed her coal-black eyes and glared at Hahoola<u>who</u> with an intense hatred. She clenched her fists as she stood beside her chestnut mare. Steam seemed to rise from her red, hot face. Not from the ninety degree heat, but from Hahoola<u>who</u>'s sharp words. She took in a couple of deep breaths while keeping her eyes pinned on the muscular boy sitting chief-like on his gleaming stallion.

Hahoola<u>who</u> let loose a shrilling yell, turned his horse, and galloped off.

Spupaleena kicked the dirt with her moccasin-covered foot. "*Kewa* ("Yes"), I will enter, and I will win." She took a deep breath and let it escape slowly. She stroked Rainbow's long, sleek neck as she peered though the tall pine trees overlooking the Columbia River. She clutched the lead rope and led her mare away. The fringe on her doeskin dress swooshed to her fast-paced stride.

She knew Rainbow had heart and would do whatever was asked of her, but deep down, Spupaleena realized her brave mare could never beat Hahoolawho's powerful stallion. The red roan, Quiy Sket—meaning Black Rain—beat every rival thus far. The stallion was known to be colossal, coming like a thief in the night. He washed his opponent away in his powerful current. Those who witnessed him stood, astonished. Spupaleena shivered at the reality of his might.

Stopping in the shade of a patch of fir trees, Spupaleena closed her eyes and buried her face in Rainbow's mane. "Creator God, I know your power, and I know all things can come to pass with you in the lead. I ask you right now to lead me down the right path, your path, in Jesus's name. *Lim lumt* ("Thank you")."

Praying gave her a peace and courage, but she knew she needed to come up with a plan. She would have to do her part, not expecting God to hand her a win with little effort. As Spupaleena pictured Quiy Sket in her mind, she saw how commanding he stood. His shoulders and hindquarters reflected massive, steel-like muscle. Hahoolawho and Quiy Sket won every race for the last three years. But Spupaleena knew there was a way—there had to be. She knew the arrogance of Hahoolawho and his family needed to be silenced.

"Are you ready, daughter?" **Skumhist** ("Black Bear") asked, snapping Spupaleena out of her galloping imagination.

"What?"

"I asked if you're ready."

"For what?"

"You need to focus on our work and not your dreams of racing, my daughter. We have deer hides to clean. They're soaking, ready to stretch and scrape. I'll ask again. Are you ready?" Skumhist drew in an impatient breath and slowly blew it out of his mouth. He had to pull her away from mindless distractions all too often.

His daughter was always daydreaming, even as a young child. She would sit by the fire in the winter months, fantasizing in her own little world, not speaking for hours at a time and dreaming away the dark, winter evenings. Her eyes would be glazed over by a cloud of make-believe. Only she could see the vibrant colors of her adventures.

"Kewa, *mistum* ("Father"), I need to put Rainbow away, and then I'll meet you." Spupaleena led her mare up the grassy hill and into her corral. "We will ride later," she whispered to her partner. Rainbow nickered. The two had an unusual bond. Rainbow seemed to know her rider's thoughts and feelings. The mare leaned her velvety brown muzzle into the crook of her owner's neck. Spupaleena giggled and rubbed its softness for a brief moment before returning to work.

"**_Lthkickha_** ("Older Sister"), I heard Hahoolawho bragging about his last win," **Pekam** ("Bobcat") announced to his sister. "He is proud and needs to be ripped off his horse." Pekam, an eleven-year-old ball of fire, acted like he was the one ousting the enemy off his stallion.

Spupaleena shrugged. "In time, **_sintahoos_** ("Brother"), in God's time." She peered at him and his disheveled braids and shook her head.

"God's time? When's that, and what does God have to do with anything? I think this God of yours doesn't really care," Pekam snorted.

"Kewa, he does," Spupaleena said confidently. "You'll see." She ignored her brother's comment and continued to scrape her hide. She clucked to herself at his lack of faith.

The siblings worked for the rest of the afternoon quietly. Spupaleena knew her job was to prepare the soil for the rain, and God would bring in that rain and harvest. She smiled as she worked, nearly tasting the sweetness of victory.

As she worked, Spupaleena's thoughts drifted back to Phillip and Elizabeth Gardner, her beloved white family south and across the river. This was a segment in her life that changed her heart forever. Just four years earlier, Spupaleena, then a tender thirteen-years-old, had a falling-out with her older sister, **Hamis-hamis** ("Morning Dove"). Years of pain and guilt exploded in a fraction of a moment. In the early hours of the morning, she had run off into a blizzard, blinded by her own fury and foolishness. She fell down a ravine, broken and bruised, and left for dead by her own demise. Spupaleena slammed her head against a boulder and hardly remembered anything, which she was thankful for.

Spupaleena later realized how much God had his hand on her the entire time by sending Phillip. He was a trapper at the time who was diligently checking his trap lines and found her a couple days later, a bloody mess, and had taken her across the river to his pregnant wife who had a knack for healing. Phillip was unnerved when he discovered the snow-covered body. He dropped his gear and ran the best he could, considering he had snowshoes strapped on to his heavy boots. He knelt down and to his dismay uncovered a young native girl. He immediately checked for any sign of life, which there was. He thanked God and got busy assembling a make-shift travois to get her home—to his home and wife.

Elizabeth welcomed the girl with unconditional love and patient care-giving methods. Spupaleena remembered her soothing voice and gentle touch. She giggled at the thought of the way Elizabeth hummed as she dressed her bandages or stirred her mouth watering stew. After many months of agonizing pain, Elizabeth nursed her back to health with various herbal concoctions, some of which Spupaleena recalled tasting mighty rancid. She not only helped to heal the girl physically but led her to Jesus, who healed her spiritually and emotionally.

Spupaleena eventually gave her heart to Jesus, and with his forgiveness and grace decided, when she was fit for travel, it would be time to head home and do some forgiving of her own. The thrill of mercy ran up and down her spine; she could imagine the look of shock on her sister's face as she expressed her regret. She could hardly contain a smile, wondering if that was wrong. As she recalled that glorious day she made her decision to follow Christ, shivers tingled through her arms and neck up to the top of her tightly braided head. It was one of the most important decisions she made in her young life.

Not soon after Spupaleena was settled in did Phillip discover his traps had been stolen, which was unheard of in those days. He decided to trek in three feet of snow for new supplies to the nearest town of Lincoln. Once he met up with his friend Hal, they set out in the blackness of a frigid, December morning, planning to be away for only a few days. Surprisingly, thieves attacked and killed Hal and left Phillip for dead. The anguish on Elizabeth's face when she was told the horrific news, would be forever burned in Spupaleena's memory.

Thankfully, an old mountain man, Bunker, found Phillip and took him to the doctor in Lincoln. He was able to locate the Gardners' cabin with help from the doctor and report to Elizabeth on Phillip's condition. Elizabeth sobbed; nearly fainting when Bunker shared the news of her husband's amputated leg. Spupaleena let a tear of her own escape as she recalled her friend's sorrow. Bunker was at a loss for words in a woman's world. But he was kind enough to stay on a couple of days to chop some more wood and make sure the women had ample food and water.

Spupaleena chuckled at the memory of old Bunker. He was rugged-looking, yet a tender, giving gentleman. His heart was in the right place as he shabbily nailed together the unfinished bassinet for the newborn baby before he left the cabin.

Spupaleena's mood turned cold as her thoughts turned to the night the baby came. As the news about Phillip's near death experience stumbled out of the old mountains man's cracked lips, Elizabeth felt a deep pain and knew it was time for the baby to come. Spupaleena panicked as her sister had always assisted with birthing duties in her village. Elizabeth walked the girl through the process and when all was said and done, a healthy baby girl named Hannah Marie was settled in her mother's arms.

Spupaleena felt like a proud parent as she pictured the newborn's fragile, long fingers in her mind. She could smell the freshness of soft, pink skin after giving Hannah a bath and hear the little cooing sounds she would make. She missed that baby. She missed Elizabeth and their early morning talks. This year's harsh winter made traveling nearly impossible so she was unable to see the Gardners since last fall.

Taking in a deep breath, Spupaleena realized she had been mesmerized by her memories. More tears trickled down her tanned cheek as she stared into the past. Her gaze slowly moved down to her sticky hands resting on her lap, and she was suddenly aware of how long she had been lost in her thoughts. The hide she had been working on was nearly done. She washed the gooey brain soup off her hands that was used to tan the hides. She never did like the rank smell that hung in the air like a dead varmint.

She took a long drink of cool water, which left Spupaleena feeling refreshed after working up a sweat not only from the vigorous work but remembering and regretting. Her emotions exploded in all directions as her mind lingered on the events of her past with the Gardners and the sorrowful death of Hamis-hamis; she struggled to cut them off.

It was late spring when Spupaleena finally made her way home from her stay with the Gardners. She was ready to ask Hamis-hamis for forgiveness, only to learn of her sister's death. She fought back tears pooling in her eyes, reminding herself that one's own pity was hardly the answer. God had been working in her, and she was learning to forgive herself—a process that seemed to take forever. Her heart ripped open and dried up like the stiff deer hide lying on the dirt before her. However, she willed herself to focus on God and his strength, not her own weakness, knowing she was made strong by him and him alone.

Eventually, Spupaleena learned that Hamis-hamis was mortified when the decision to halt the search for her sister was made. Hamis-hamis felt torn apart, grieving for weeks over their years of fighting and her harsh

Carmen Peone

words, questioning what kind of sister she had been. She cried and chastised herself, begging the Creator for forgiveness. She knew Spupaleena deserved better treatment, protection perhaps. Yes, she should have protected her little sister not belittle her every waking moment. Jealousy fueled Hamis-hamis's anger; in the end, it only shamed her.

The worst of it was yet to come. Spupaleena felt she would never recover from her beloved grandmother's death. It was only a few days after the search for her ended when **Sneena** ("Owl"), passed away. She was old and frail. Her time on earth was done, leaving one life to go on to another. It was almost too much for Hamis-hamis and Skumhist. The two grieved together and comforted one another. They prayed and sweat for several days for the return of their beloved Spupaleena.

Months passed with no indication that she was alive. The family came to the conclusion that she would never return to them. No one could live out in the freezing weather that long. But with no body to bury was imaginable. What would they do? How would they let go and find any hint of closure?

Life went on.

Hamis-hamis was convinced that everything was her fault. She refused to forgive herself. Worry and stress led to pneumonia, and during the coldest month of winter, she joined her grandmother in death. Skumhist, now tired and weary, was left to raise his energetic son by himself. His heart was shattered, left for the buzzards to pick at what little remained. Family helped with the boy as Skumhist continued to trap and collect his pelts. He merely went through the motions, numb to the living. He struggled to get up each morning, strapping on his snowshoes, and fighting the frigid, snow-filled mountains to check his traps.

Finally, the end of spring had come to pass, and the sun warmed the earth. The time came to deliver harvested pelts to the Great Falls up the Columbia River where Indians traded with the *soo ya pee* ("White Man"). The morning was warm and bright, and the sky seemed to display a deeper blue than normal. Skumhist had been sorting his pelts, organizing them for travel. Hearing a commotion, he stood and looked up. His cousin was running at him, waving his arms and hollering, "She's alive!"

At first, Skumhist was confused. He stood frozen. Who was alive? What was his relative so excited about? **It Huẖ Pa Pa Latsa** ("Sleeping Moose") had stopped in front of Skumhist, out of breath and panting. Sweat ran down the sides of his face, and he was jumping up and down like a small child.

"What is it?" Skumhist asked, somewhat annoyed. He was in a hurry to get on the trail to the falls. He was eager to fish, tired of the winter-dried meat and berries, yet feeling empty without his daughter. Having her cheer him on made him feel like he could out-fish everyone. But now his attitude was different. He cared less how many salmon he speared; fishing this year would be different without his daughter. Pekam could do the rest. He was young and ready to take over and let his father rest and wallow in his what-ifs.

"She's alive!" It <u>Huh</u> Pa Pa Latsa repeated. "She's at the Great Falls. She's coming home." He waved his arms as he excitedly looked around to the relatives standing nearby.

Skumhist dropped the pelts he had been holding and fell to his knees. His head spun like an eddy in a stream. He could hardly breathe. Trembling, he thanked the Creator though tears that streamed down his hot cheeks. His relations had cheered with joy and had helped him gather his bounty so they could all head out as quickly as possible. Skumhist trembled at the thought of holding his daughter once again in his sturdy arms. Suddenly, the fur smelled fresher, somewhat energizing. He quickly stood, lifting his hands to the deep blue sky in gratitude.

His heart felt like it would beat straight out of his chest. He was dizzy, moving slowly, trying to place one foot in front of the other and remain upright. Skumhist never knew happiness like what he felt at that moment. His daughter was returning to him. He felt peace. He felt overjoyed. He felt alive for the first time in months.

Chapter 2

Spupaleena gasped as her eyes locked in on her tear-stricken father racing toward her as she plodded along riding her tired mare. Her heart beat so hard she thought it would jump right out of her skin. She was just south of the Great Falls, barely able to hear the thundering water spill over the horseshoe rock walls. She saw Skumhist running and yelling her name, tears streaming down his face. She jumped off Rainbow, dropping the reins and sprinting to him. They embraced, hugging and crying, and Spupaleena buried her face into her father's chest. Skumhist held his daughter tightly, afraid to let go only to lose her again.

There was much catching up to do and many stories to share. She yearned to tell her mistum about Phillip and Elizabeth and her newfound God. Her stomach flittered about like a grasshopper in a jar. She needed to see Hamis-hamis and Sneena. She had anticipated holding Pekam once again, never taking anyone for granted—ever.

After the initial reunion, they all headed to the falls. The sun dropped behind splashes of orange and purple. The moon was a mere sliver, allowing a canopy of stars to sparkle against the blackened sky.

"I can't wait to see Hamis-hamis and **Stimteema** ("Grandmother"), where are they?" Spupaleena eagerly searched the people.

"Let's just unload these pelts and set up camp," Skumhist said, his voice as solemn as the expression on his face. He tried to hide his anxious behavior, but the palms of his hands sweat so badly, he struggled to hold onto the slick pelts. Wiping his hands on his buckskin pants was no help. He was just too nervous.

Spupaleena stood and nodded. A questioning look covered her face. Even though endless words reeled through her head, she kept silent. Were they hurt? Sick? Why did she not see them? Her heart ached and now so did the pit in her stomach. The right time would come to speak with her father. She would spend the time unpacking in prayer.

Skumhist dreaded telling his daughter the sad news of her sister and grandmother. He knew his daughter would be torn. Spupaleena's love for her grandmother was endless. Her heart would shatter like a broken vase. Skumhist hated to see his daughter in any kind of agony. He was tired of pain and sorrow but knew he needed to break the news to her—the sooner the better.

It was late before they were able to eat some dried meat and bannock. Father and daughter sat by a lifeless fire. Spupaleena patiently waited for her father to share what was heavy on his heart. Fear sparked once again as thoughts of her tima possibly being gravely sick swirled in her mind. *Was something terribly wrong?* She sat patiently, sipping her rosehip tea and staring into the glowing embers. She missed the smooth, sweet tea. All she could do was sit and blow at the steam swirling from her cup as she willed her body to remain still, fighting off waves of tremors attempting to take over.

Finally, her father spoke. "Spupaleena…"

"Kewa, mistum," she whispered, afraid to look him in the face. Her body shook with anticipation.

"I have some bad news. I don't know how to tell you this…" he said, shaking his head. A tear rolled down his saddened face as he sat, staring at the palms of his sweaty hands. He fought back the lump in his throat.

They sat in silence as Skumhist collected his thoughts. Finally, he had the nerve to speak.

"Your sister and grandmother have passed on—"

"*Loot!* ("No")," Spupaleena shouted and jumped to her feet. "Loot!" She shook her head in disbelief. Her entire body shuddered, and her heart pounded as she tried to catch her breath.

"Kewa, I'm sorry." Skumhist stood and gathered his daughter into his strong, sturdy arms. He let her sob, tears streaking his buckskin shirt. Silently, he held her tight, stroking her hair. She had never known this kind of compassion from him before, but she needed it and invited more. She had welcomed his caring and love; she needed his strength. *Thank you, Father, for giving my mistum back to me,* she prayed silently. She squeezed him tightly, not wanting to let go.

After awhile, they pulled apart and sat back down. Spupaleena looked into her father's grief-stricken eyes. She quickly glanced down, so distraught she could hardly speak. Skumhist went on to share the incidents with Spupaleena. They cried and comforted one another late into the night, knowing the following day it would be over, and work would begin. Life would go back to normal, but their hearts would remain shattered. It was just the way things were.

Spupaleena saddled Rainbow, ready to exercise her in the nearby hills. She was finished brooding over the sorrow of the past. Today, she was ready to walk again in the brightness of the present, even daring to look forward and see what God had in store for her. She would proceed one step at a time; one prayer at a time.

The early morning felt cool and crisp. The sun was just beginning to peek over the eastern mountains. She was refreshed and ready to ride, knowing her time was limited. Skumhist had instructed her to return early in order to finish the hides that were still soaking and ready to stretch. She realized her father merely tolerated her horse passion.

"When I win, mistum will change his thinking," she mumbled, sliding her hands down the length of her braids. She placed her foot into the stirrup, careful not to jab the side of her mare.

Swinging her leg over the saddle, she whirled around and trotted off. There were just a few days before her first real race; the pair needed to be ready. For three years now, Spupaleena had set up various racing courses with her friends, but only as a training tool. Her mare was strong and consistent, always giving her heart to her owner. The pair won most of those contests, but the opposition was against middle-aged family horses, most of which were stallions. Rainbow was no doubt in good shape and in perfect health but not good enough to match the horses running in the more competitive races. Those horses were taller, younger, and faster. Something needed to change; a new horse, perhaps. Spupaleena had no idea how that would happen, but she had to find a way. She would take it to God and let him work out the details in his timing and according to his will.

Fortunately, the upcoming event was more endurance than speed. Rainbow would hardly break a sweat. The pair rode miles a day up and down the forested hills, not only at a long trot, but a nice, steady canter. On the grassy, straight stretches where there were no gopher holes to stumble over, she would let her mare take the reins and gallop for a bit. Rainbow was prepared, and her bottom line showed it. Her flank was tight, and her hind end was a solid mass like a child's marble.

She rode up to her brother flashing a smile as she pulled Rainbow to a halt.

Pekam looked up and grinned back at her. "Lthkickha, I will ride with you when I finish this last pelt," he said.

"Kewa, I'll meet you down by the creek." She looked around, squinting her eyes against the afternoon sun. "It's warmer, and the grass is dryer. Rainbow won't slip around like she did yesterday."

"How's her leg?"

"She's okay. There's no heat on either of her back legs; she'll be fine." Spupaleena nodded. "Good work, sintahoos."

"Lim lumt, I'll be there as soon as I can." He looked up, flashing a tooth-filled smile at his sister. Black dirt covered his tanned face, making his teeth and the whites of his eyes gleam brightly.

Spupaleena nodded and walked her mare toward the river. She had enough time to slowly warm up Rainbow to avoid further injuries. The spring, mushy weather allowed for gloomy ground conditions. They had taken a couple of steps, and the mare was already sliding, digging in her hooves to stay upright.

"I hate this slick clay." She patted her mare's neck. "It's slicker than a snake sheddin' its skin." She let the animal pick her way over the ground until they reached sandier terrain.

The next morning, Spupaleena headed out at the crack of dawn to meet with Phillip and Elizabeth. She had found a section of the Columbia River a horse could easily swim to the other side. The spot was only a few miles downriver, and she could be at the Gardner's place by late morning. She took it easy at first, but once Rainbow expressed her desire to pick up speed, off they went.

The hours passed quickly, and in no time, the cabin came in to view. Spupaleena caught sight of Elizabeth as she crouched in her garden attacking weeds while humming quietly, soaking up the warmth of the sun as it tingled up and down the length of her back. Hannah sat right beside her, twig in hand, mimicking her mother.

"Wi, family." Spupaleena broke out into a grin as she approached her beloved friends.

"Hello to you too." Elizabeth stood and wiped her hands on her apron. She was three months pregnant with her and Phillip's third child and barely showing.

Spupaleena reined her mare to a stop and gracefully slid off. The two ladies hugged, and four-year-old Hannah ran as fast as she could to greet her aunt, braids flapping in rhythm to each step. Spupaleena picked her up as the little girl squealed in delight.

"I missed you, Auntie Spuppy!" Hannah held on tight, rubbing her chubby little hands along Spupaleena's waist-long braids. It never bothered Spupaleena when tiny clumps of dirt were later found as she unbraided her hair; knowing from where they came simply warmed her heart.

"I love you too." They twirled around in circles, giggling like they were both little girls until dizziness overcame them.

"How have you been? You look strong and confident today," Elizabeth commented as they placed their arms around each other, walking to the cabin. Hannah slid down and ran ahead, hollering for her papa.

"I do feel strong; I'm ready for this next race." Spupaleena's face glowed.

"When is it?" Phillip asked as he approached, arms open.

"Wi, brother. In four days." Phillip hugged Spupaleena.

Spupaleena glanced around. "Where's Delbert?"

"Asleep. He plum run himself ragged chasing after each bug and critter he could find. I don't know how many rocks he overturned in search of every last one." Elizabeth shook her head, laughing at the image. Delbert, now a year and a half, had his grandfather's reddish hair and big green eyes.

The group headed into the cabin, seeking shade and a bite to eat. Sitting down, Spupaleena's mood quickly changed. "I'm ready to put the evil snake in the dirt," she said, her eyes narrowing in disgust.

Hannah came in, settling herself on Spupaleena's lap and clutching her baby doll by the leg.

"You sound angry. What's behind it?" Phillip asked.

Spupaleena shrugged her shoulders, fingering the doll's raggedy hair. "Everyone thinks I'm just a silly little girl who will make a fool of herself."

"Spup." Elizabeth placed her hand on the girl's shoulder. "People will always talk. Women normally don't compete like you do. You have to learn to deal with it." Elizabeth paused a moment before continuing. "But let me ask you this: Why are you racing? Who are you really riding for?" Her voice was soft and gentle.

Spupaleena pursed her lips and looked Elizabeth square in the eyes. "I'm riding to prove that I can. To once and for all quiet the mouths of those who merely wag their tongues with—"

"Spup," Phillip interrupted. He leaned on his walking stick, shifting his weight from his wooden leg to his good one, keeping his eyes locked on hers.

"*Who* are you riding for?" Phillip asked softly yet firmly.

"I'm riding to defend my honor, to let these so-called warriors know I'm worthy to race with them—against them." Her voice grew louder as she spoke. Hannah looked up at Spupaleena with round, anxious eyes. Spupaleena glanced down, giving the scared youngster a soft, reassuring squeeze.

"We understand." Elizabeth smiled, attempting to support and calm her friend down. "I know you love riding and the feeling of competing with others. I love your spirit of courage, but again, think of *who* you are really riding for. Who will get the glory of it all?" Elizabeth took Spupaleena's hands in her own. "Who do you want to have it?"

Spupaleena looked down, feeling sheepish, realizing her friends were right. A rush of crimson flushed her face. She needed to race for God and him alone. But Hahoolawho was in for a lesson, and she was sure God would allow her the honor. She would just have to keep those thoughts to herself.

Spupaleena glanced down at Hannah's delicate hands enfolded in her own. "God will always be first in my heart." She nodded. "He'll always be first in my heart.

Carmen Peone

You're right, lim lumt." She looked first at Elizabeth and then at Phillip. "But know this: Hahoola<u>who</u> will only be humbled when he loses." Spupaleena winked, and they all burst out laughing.

"Yes, he will," Phillip agreed. "We will be praying for you and your safety and attitude." He chuckled again. Phillip learned long ago that Spupaleena could be pushed only so far. Otherwise, she would run full speed ahead into making decisions by emotion rather than reason.

"I know you will." Spupaleena hugged Hannah and tickled her belly, making the child giggle and squeal in an attempt to hide her embarrassment. Phillip and Elizabeth smiled at each other. Just the other day, they were talking about how Spupaleena had grown from a misplaced seed swirling in the breeze to a well-rooted sunflower—bright and shining.

Anger still surged through Spupaleena's veins when she thought about Hahoola<u>who</u> but would admit to nothing. For a bit, she played with Hannah, trying her best to fake a sense of playfulness. But her thoughts whirled around in her head, and she had a hard time concentrating on their tea party.

"What's wrong, Auntie Spuppy?" Hannah poured a cup of pretend tea, humming "Jesus Loves Me."

Spupaleena looked at her, the heat of surprise climbing up her neck. "Oh, nothing my little, precious one." Spupaleena wrinkled her nose and brushed her finger against the little girl's pink, pudgy cheek. "This is really tasty tea, and the biscuits are delicious."

"Thank you. I'm making some cake, like Mama. Would you like some?" Hannah's little voice was sweet and innocent.

"Kewa, a big one. Traveling all this way has made me so hungry." Spupaleena winked at the child as she handed a pretend piece of cake to her. She could never remain upset as long as Hannah's dancing eyes and bright smile looked up at her so innocent and full of love. Her dimpled cheeks alone were enough to scare off anything but delight.

"Perhaps we should eat some real food," Elizabeth said, setting down her plate. Hannah frowned as her bottom lip protruded. Elizabeth gave her a quick hug.

"Then we can talk horses after." Phillip rubbed his hands together and shot her a quirky look. "I have a new idea to share with you," he said.

Spupaleena nodded in delight. Horse talk, her favorite kind.

"Rainbow just can't beat those faster, bigger horses," Spupaleena said, kicking at the dirt inside the corral. Her face filled with concern. "She has only run against **Simillkameen** ("Swan") and **Qualkhun's** ("Porcupine") horses.

Phillip slipped a strand of hay in his mouth and nodded. He thought a moment.

"Instead of kicking for speed, I made you this whip to tap on her rump. It will extend her stride in the front end. She'll reach forward, and her speed will increase."

Phillip chuckled. "Sammy didn't think it was such a great idea at first, but his stride lengthened tremendously the further we rode."

Spupaleena took the whip in her hand. She held the wooden handle, a nice fit. She let her fingers glide along the soft, leather braid. "This won't sting her?" She felt uneasy.

"No, the leather is short so the pop will be soft but get her attention and claim her speed."

She shrugged her shoulders. "Okay, I'll give it a try." Spupaleena tapped the whip at Phillip's wooden leg. "Faster!" she teased.

Phillip laughed, taking his Stetson off and waving it at her and then grew serious again. "Let the first few strokes just touch her at a walk and trot so she knows it's there." He made the intended movements with his own hands.

Spupaleena stood, tapping the whip in her open palm. "I'm sure she'll figure it out fairly quick." She snickered.

"Yeah, then let her full-out gallop and tap her lightly. Increase the taps slightly with each stride and feel her reach her legs forward." Phillip raised his eyebrows. "You'll see."

"Are you sure?" She slapped the whip against her leg and winced. "That'll leave a bruise." She tried to rub away the sting.

"Come on, their hide is much tougher than ours. Don't be a...*o<u>h</u>uh teelut* ("Baby")."

"A what? Where did you learn that?"

Phillip just smiled.

"Oh, one more thing, God said those who have ears, let them hear." Phillip grabbed the whip out of her hand, whooping and hollering, chasing Spupaleena around the corral until they were both panting and dropped to the ground in laughter. Spupaleena felt like a little girl; she had not had that much fun in a long time.

Delbert must have woke up to all the commotion. Elizabeth carried the sleepy-eyed boy over to the corral while Hannah bolted past, running ahead of them. He clapped his hands, showing a huge tooth-scattered grin at the site of his papa.

"What are you two doing out here?" Elizabeth stared at them, shaking her head in disbelief. "You two are filthy. And smell just as bad!"

Phillip and Spupaleena looked at each other and again broke out laughing. They were covered in mud like two hogs rolling around, keeping the flies at bay.

Spupaleena lowered her gaze to the whip and thought, *Kewa, I'll use this on that evil snake and see how fast he can run.* She smiled only to herself this time.

"You can win this race, <u>l</u>thkickha, I know you can," Pekam said, hoisting a saddle over Rainbow's back.

"She feels strong; she's ready," Spupaleena said. She rubbed a Nettle liniment over the animal's back, neck, and legs in a slow and deliberate, circular motion, praying as she went. She asked for God's healing and protection.

"You don't need your God's protection. You're strong enough," Pekam hopped up and down, stopping briefly to stretch as if he was the jockey.

"Someday, sintahoos, you will know." Spupaleena worked without even a sideways glance at her brother. Tossing the unused solution into the bushes, she then set the wooden bowl down.

Pekam shook his head. "Come on, everyone else is ready and lining up." He grabbed Rainbow's reins and led her away.

"I'll be there in a minute." Spupaleena knelt down and tightened the laces on her moccasins then adjusted her clothing so everything was secure—one less concern. One last time, she ran her hands down her braids as if to steady her nerves.

Pekam led the calm horse through the gathering crowd. "One would think the bets would be better than this," he mumbled. "<u>L</u>thkickha is worth blankets, beads, and furs, not pots and spoons." His face reddened with disgust.

"I'm ready now," Spupaleena said, her voice strong and confident. She had been watching her mare's reaction to all of the ongoing commotion. Rainbow's calm sense of self was her greatest strength.

Pekam fixed his eyes on his sister's freshly braided hair, and a smile crossed his face. "You can win. Ride hard, <u>l</u>thkickha!" Pekam stepped aside, nearly being run over by a boy trotting up, yelling at Spupaleena.

"I will beat you so badly you will cry all the way back to your mistum."

The crowd whooped and hollered as Spupaleena's face turned crimson. Her eyes closed to mere slits. "If you think your horse is so fast, make your bet, big mouth." She shook her fist at him. Then, realizing her emotions grabbed the reins, she let her arms slip to her sides. She took in a deep breath and let it out slowly, trying to extinguish her anger.

The crowd went silent. Only the thumping hooves of the dancing horses could be heard as they picked up on the excitement of their riders. Yet, Rainbow stood with one back leg cocked. Pekam rubbed his hands together, holding back his seething anger. He wanted to pull the boy off his gelding and stomp on his chest. But he knew his sister would chastise him. *We don't fight with our fists*, she would instruct him. *We fight with honor and wit, which comes from God.* Pekam doubted the idea of including God, but he loved his sister as much as she loved her God; he would honor her wishes.

"I bet him." The boy pointed down at his gelding as the animal twirled about. The crowd caught their breath. Mumbling ricocheted down the rows of onlookers. Never before had a rider put up his horse for a wager. No one had ever been that foolish.

Spupaleena glanced over her shoulder, spotting her brother. His eyes seemed to spark as he energetically shook his head in disbelief. His smile communicated the idiotic notion of his sister's competitor. He turned his back, clapping his hands in one single motion, trying his hardest to contain his exhilaration. He was elated at the prospect of a new horse.

Spupaleena stared at the boy square in the face. His glare sharpened. Finally, Spupaleena nodded. "Kewa, I accept your offer." She tilted her head and raised her brows, astonished at his dim-wittedness.

"Get ready to crawl back home, foolish girl." The boy sneered, then turned and went to line up.

Spupaleena laughed. She turned her mare and readied herself for the faint cry at the end of the mile-long stretch of grass that would start the race. The boy lined up his prancing horse next to hers. Even though Rainbow stood still, Spupaleena could feel the mare was on edge and ready to lurch forward at her rider's command.

"I will see you at the finish line," he barked.

Spupaleena ignored his snide remark. She refused to play in to his game. She focused on the race. She felt Rainbow tense in anticipation. Feeling her own tightness, she took in a deep breath, held it a second, then let it rush out through her mouth as she sank into the saddle, one hand loose on the rein and ready to be thrown forward, the other tightly clutching the whip. Then in moments came the shrilling cry.

Chapter 3

Spupaleena threw back her arm and let the end of her newly acquired whip cross Rainbow's rump. The mare lunged forward, her nostrils flaring. Her eyes and ears pointed ahead. Determination sped throughout her body. She would run for her owner whom she loved and trusted.

Dirt spattered the onlookers, and hooves pounded the earth. Spupaleena was so focused she failed to hear the screaming voices of those cheering her on. She could feel Rainbow's heart thumping against her legs and see the heat rising from her sweat-covered body as they dashed around a corner.

Spupaleena saw the boy out of the corner of her eye but refused to look in his direction. She gave Rainbow the increasing swats as Phillip had instructed. Rainbow stretched with her legs and neck, pushing with her hind end, crossing the horsehair finish line a half of a length in front of her competitor. The two men that had been holding the finish rope looked at one another, shook their heads in amazement, and just stood there motionless.

The remaining racers flew past the finish rope, slowed their horses down, and finally turned them around, trotting back down the course allowing their winded horses to cool off. Spupaleena held her head high as Rainbow pranced like she was carrying royalty. When they reached their perspective piles of bartered loot, Spupaleena claimed not her meager mound of prizes but the one standing in defeat. The boy slid off his horse and handed her the reins.

His father rushed up, yelling at his son and belittling his foolishness. The boy hung his head, not even peeking for one last glance at his horse. He said not a word. His father grabbed him by his shirt and hauled him off. Spupaleena sat in the saddle motionless, watching the boy walk off. She almost felt bad.

"You did it!" Pekam patted her leg as it dangled off the side of her horse. She soon forgot the sadness and collected her winnings. Pekam snatched the rein out of his sister's hand and led the prized horse away. Spupaleena followed, leading her mare as the crowd cheered, especially the women, who patted her back as she strode by them, smiling in victory. She felt pride like never before, and it felt good. For once, she was someone—someone who made a difference, and someone others looked up to.

Conceit filled her full as she silently thanked God for her well-earned triumph. Funny thing was, the more she prayed, the more empty and alone she felt.

She shrugged it off and caught up to her brother. *I'm the winner*, she thought. *I earned it.*

"We must now name my trophy." She smiled brightly at Pekam. "Any suggestions?"

"What do we name this stocky Appaloosa?" He teased in a funny voice. "How about Red Moon or Spotted Wind?" Pekam laughed, and Spupaleena couldn't help herself. She swatted him with her whip as they darted around the horses.

"Spotted Wind? I'm not sure about that, sintahoos," she said over her shoulder. "We'll think of something majestic." She stopped in front of the newly acquired gelding, panting and leaning her hands on her knees, looking him in his big, black eye. "Thank you for your help." She turned to look at her brother and flashed him a look of appreciation.

"Kewa…" Pekam blushed; he had no idea why but felt embarrassed nonetheless.

"Okay then, rub down Rainbow and turn them both out. After that, finish scraping my hides and—"

"Loot! I will take care of your horses but never do your chores. Nice try," Pekam stated, knowing his sister was teasing him. He chuckled, grabbing a handful of grass, and rubbed the horses down, singing a traditional warrior song as he worked.

Phillip and Elizabeth sat down for their evening meal. Spupaleena had been heavy on their hearts. Bowing their heads, Phillip prayed, "Father God, we thank you for our many blessings and the food you provide us. We thank you for our daily dose of grace. We also come to you asking for wisdom for our sister, Spupaleena. We know you are working in her heart as she grows and learns. Give her direction, Father God, and let us help her in any way we can. In Jesus's mighty name, amen." Elizabeth and Hannah echoed the amen and passed the food around.

"I know she won again, and I heard word that she won a new colt," Phillip said. He took a bite of steak.

Elizabeth nodded. "Yeah, I'm afraid she's going to get too big for her britches."

"Well, she may; she's a gifted rider. I hope she keeps her focus on God. She's too good to mess it up." He took a sip of steaming coffee.

"I agree. She's so talented. I want to see her succeed. I think she still blames herself for her sister's death. I know something still haunts her."

Phillip put his fork down and wiped his mouth. "Me too. Maybe you could go see her…talk to her. You have a way of getting her to see things your way."

"Not my way."

Phillip smiled. "No, not your way, but still, the right way." He winked at his wife. She smiled back, catching his gaze for a moment. "God will take care of things. We just need to love and support her," he said.

As dusk rolled in, brilliant hues of purple and blue swept across the skyline. A hushed silence settled over the valley as the natives settled in for the night. Spupaleena sat outside on a fallen log, listening to the chorus of crickets echoing throughout the woods. She watched the stars glimmer, recalling the day's race and her success.

She was satisfied with Rainbow but knew it was the mare's last run, which saddened her. She felt like she was betraying her loyal partner.

But now, with the four-year-old Appaloosa she had just won, they would fly. A chill traveled up and down her spine like an electric bolt. She knew he had more in him; the boy just had no idea how to ride—not enough skills physically nor mentally. She could see willingness in the gelding, and she would teach him love and respect. She visualized them crossing the finish rope with ease; he could travel twice the length of Rainbow and not break a sweat.

Skumhist stood behind his daughter. "You have won again, I hear," he said with distain.

Spupaleena jumped as her father's voice jerked her out of her fantasy. "Kewa, Mistum, I won, and my prize is in the corral." She tossed a twig aside, trying her best to remain respectful. The more her father loathed her training, the harder it was.

"When are you going to stop this?" He crossed his arms in front of his chest. "You and Pekam cost me today. I needed help with the pelts and hides. I want this done before we leave for the Kettle Falls; I don't want to rush around like the lazy men do."

"Mistum"—Spupaleena kept her voice soft and controlled, although her blood ran wild through her veins—"racing is what I want to do. Horses…they're my life. Please, mistum, let me have my dreams—"

"Loot! They're useless; you can't eat a blanket or pots and pans or any other winnings. You need to get serious and put in a respectful day's work, not bring home another horse to feed." Skumhist's neck and face were red, and his veins looked as though they would burst right out of his neck and forehead. Spupaleena thought he would surely explode.

"I will feed and care for them, you won't. Pekam—"

"Pekam, kewa, you have dragged that boy into this. I need help, and now all he talks about are your horses." Skumhist stood over his daughter. His agitation festered into rage. Fear and frustration continued to plague him. His daughter was so bullheaded.

Skumhist drew in a breath and let it out slowly. He dropped his arms to his sides and spoke softly yet firmly. "I will not argue with you, *stumpkeelt* ("Daughter"). My wishes must be taken seriously. This is the end of it." He turned and strode off; he was in no mood for irrational behavior.

Spupaleena was crushed. Turning around, she picked up a fist full of dirt and threw it as far as she could. Tears streamed down her hot face. "I will *not* stop." She picked up pinecone after pinecone and hurled them into the darkness; better to take out her anger on dead, fallen cones than her beloved but infuriating father. When the steam finally blew out, she glanced down at her hands. There was enough light glowing through the scattered clouds that she could see the scrapes and blood.

Spupaleena knelt on the ground and bowed her head. "Father God, please forgive me. What's wrong with wanting victories? Of wanting good things, to be as good as the men? You made me who I am; you placed these desires in me of raising and racing horses. Why can't I? Are you stopping me? Why? *Why* would you give me these feelings to only rip them away? I ask for the path you want me to take. I ask that it be clear to me, Father. I ask that mistum will accept it. In Jesus's name, lim lumt. Amen."

For the next few days, Spupaleena did as her father requested, working horses only when she finished with the day's tasks. Most girls her age were already married or were about to be. She was thankful Skumhist had not brought it up, at least not yet. Boys were her competition, not her attraction, even at her tender age.

Spupaleena's anxiousness grew every hour as she scraped a rabbit pelt. Not being able to ride was killing her. Her next race was in a couple of weeks. She was mildly familiar with the new colt; they needed more time together to get a feel for one another. Skumhist was not helping. She was convinced her father drummed up chores for her to do in order to keep her away from riding. *How childish*, she thought. *How selfish*. She seethed as she worked, trying not to ruin the pelt.

A few days later while scraping a whitetail deer hide, it dawned on her that she could breed Rainbow to Jack Dalley's big paint stallion. *Why not*, she thought. Her flesh instantly broke out in goose bumps. *The mare has such a confident yet gentle mind, and Sampson's massive muscles bulge as he stands confident and regal.* Spupaleena smiled brightly at her thoughts. The 16.1-hand, solid-bodied giant was a perfect match.

The excitement sent another wave of shivers coursing through her body. She looked up with a big smile and thanked God for the dreams he placed in her heart. She knew it came from him. She had prayed for direction, and now the inspiration reeled through her mind, spinning and rearing like a spunky foal. She thought about what the colt would look like or perhaps a wide-eyed filly. Strong hindquarters, straight, thin legs, perfectly aligned neck and head—yes, all of it. The foal would be mostly black with splashes of white streaking his back and legs.

Spupaleena hoped the foal would be a colt to keep the bloodline resilient—a fine racing stock indeed. A horse ranch with many stallions would do her fine. Sampson would start it strong. A dream she could catch. *Was it too big?* she wondered. *Loot!* If God put in her heart, it would be reachable. It had to be. She fantasized as she worked. Her world expanded by the minute.

Dawn came early. The sky ran a stream of pink through its horizon. Spupaleena had tossed and turned throughout the night. She was barely able to sleep. However, her mind was made up. She had to be true to herself and what God had chosen for her. She had a choice to either live for someone else, her father, or jockey her own course. Someone would be disappointed, but today, it was not going to be Spupaleena.

After tying off her braid with a thin strip of leather, she rose to search out Skumhist. Her stomach seemed to whirl around like a twig in an eddy. She found him sitting outside his tule-pit home about to eat camas mixed with dried huckleberries.

"**Hast eel_th_ qua quost, mistum**, ("Good Morning, Father")," Spupaleena said, attempting not to sound smug. Her mouth was so dry she could hardly get the words to roll off her tongue.

Skumhist nodded, not wanting to talk with food rotating around in his mouth.

"You're up early," Skumhist said. He tore off a hunk of dried meat with his teeth and chewed on it, savoring the wild flavor.

Spupaleena made an effort to smile. "Kewa, I…" For feeling so brave earlier, she struggled to gather her courage. "I'm going to race, mistum, I know—"

"You know?" Skumhist jumped to his feet, nearly choking on the half-eaten bit of deer, staring down at his daughter in disbelief. Color drained from his face. "I thought we were done with this."

"Loot, you were done. Please listen, please," Spupaleena cried.

"To such foolishness? Loot." He shook his head.

"I want to race horses, have a ranch of my own." She choked back hot tears.

"A ranch? With useless animals? Will you raise them to eat, and what would you do with their hides?"

"To eat? Never. I would raise and sell the colts. I will train them to race and win." Spupaleena continued to fight back the tears; she refused to let her father see her weak and crying like a little one. "Mistum, please—"

"Please what? Loot, I will not approve of this. Stumpkeelt, it will never work; it's just a dream. I need you and Pekam to help me; it's how it has always been—our way of life. There is no need to change. Things are good—"

"Good? How? Good for whom? I'm only happy when I'm working and training my horses; it's what God has gifted me with. I want to raise them, and I will, I'm sorry…" Spupaleena rose. "I'm sorry," she whispered, placing her hand on his shoulder. "I'm sorry."

Skumhist nodded, his face twisted in anguish. He felt as if he had just lost his daughter all over again. All he had ever wanted was to work together with his family, where he was most happy. His daughter's decision left a heaviness that settled deep in his soul.

As Spupaleena turned and walked away, an immense weight fell off her back like never before. She hated to hurt her father—and the look on his face would burn in her mind forever—but she was miserable walking the path he expected her to take. Change had to happen. Realizing that sometimes it took courage to make that change; she knew her decision was the right one. The remainder of her life was at stake, and most importantly, her happiness.

"God, help him understand," she muttered. She released those pent-up tears; they streamed down her cheeks, and she let them. She welcomed the internal cleansing. It was a bittersweet moment. After awhile, she walked on, rubbing her face dry with the back of her hand. "It's the right thing to do." She glanced heavenward as if asking for God's reassurance.

"I'm coming with you," Pekam hollered stubbornly.

"Not this time, sintahoos." Spupaleena reached for the lead. Pekam grabbed her arm.

"Please, lthkickha, I can help you, I can—"

"*Kukneeya* ("Listen"), I want you to stay here and care for Rainbow. She still needs to be ridden, and you can help me by doing that. Besides, mistum needs you. He's sad that I'm leaving. He needs your support, and I need to be alone with God to focus and pray, to train." Spupaleena caught her brother's eyes and then quickly looked away. It turned her stomach to see him look so dejected, but she would not continue to disappoint her father—one of them had to stay.

Pekam loosened his grip on her. Spupaleena took hold of the colt's rein and led him away.

"Take care of *Nee Ap Kukneeya* ("Forever Listening")," Pekam said.

"What? Who?"

"I named him." Pekam smiled, and his round eyes glimmered in the noon sun. Spupaleena gave him a questioning look. "The others will be forever listening to his hoof beats racing in the sky of their defeated minds."

Spupaleena laughed. She shook her head. "Sintahoos, you make me proud. Nee Ap Kukneeya, it is. I like it." She gently waved her heels on the colt's sides, and off they walked. Pekam could hear his sister's faint laughter in the distance. He smiled as well, even though he was disheartened.

Once out of the village, she kicked her gelding into a gallop. This time, she was leaving for the right reasons, and she would return in a few weeks.

The sun hung low in the sky by the time Spupaleena reached her special spot. She had to climb high to get there, but glancing around, the mountains were endless as were the green parade of trees. The colt's neck and chest were lathered, but he still had plenty of energy to carry her many more miles.

There was a good deal of work to be done with the youngster, and this was the spot to make it happen. The terrain was rough, rocky, and challenging. She took one last panoramic look and slipped off her horse. The colt was as green as the spring grass surrounding her and needed a solid foundation. That was why the boy lost, she was sure. This beautiful animal was now hers, and she was ready to get to work.

Spupaleena chewed on a piece of dry deer meat before jumping on bareback. She wanted to feel his movements, and she wanted him to feel her slightest shift of seat and legs. They needed to ride as one. She recognized his willingness to please and learn. She lay on his back and rubbed him all over, sliding backward as she went and finally sliding off his rear end. He was so relaxed. She then hopped back on and circled him first to the right, then to the left, making sure he was softening and listening to her.

His ears turned back at her, not in an aggressive manner, but showing her he was listening and receptive. He simply responded to the slightest change of her legs. Spupaleena was confident she could get him ready for the race in three short weeks. He might not win, but he would not come in last. He would surprise everyone, especially the one who foolishly lost him, if he was brave enough to show his face.

"Tonight, I will be with you, Father God, and tomorrow, the real training will begin," she prayed. She rubbed the gelding down and staked him out.

Spupaleena wished she could read. Elizabeth had taught her the ABCs and a few words, but that was all. She wanted her own Bible. She knew the truth ran through its pages. Elizabeth did teach her many verses, and she had memorized each one like it was her last. The one verse she clung to lately came from Psalm 91:1, 2, which read: "Those who live in the shelter of the Most High will find rest in the shadow of the Almighty. This I declare about the Lord: He alone is my refuge, my place of safety; he is my God, and I trust him."

She would trust him with her life and plans to include *kawup* ("Horses"). She sat on a tule-mat and prayed, feeling completely safe and at peace under the twinkling canopy of stars. The sky was clear and cool, but the warmth of her dream held her tightly.

Her eyelids grew heavy as she recited different verses and prayed. The full moon lit up the heavens as she searched for her elk robe. The last thing she remembered was her second favorite verse: "In your presence is fullness of joy."

Halfway into her training, Spupaleena was galloping her colt; he felt strong and confident. They wove in and out of larch trees and were jumping smoothly over fallen logs like deer. Her balance was nearly perfect riding bareback. She felt like she was part of him. Deer and grouse would jump out of the brush, and he never flinched. She knew he would respond so effortlessly but was amazed at his progress. The animal loved and trusted his new owner; she had earned his respect with her gentle yet firm methods.

Nee Ap K̲ukneeya mirrored every movement his rider made. He was becoming softer in his mouth with every ride, which had become twice a day. Spupaleena felt as bright and light as a *pelpalwheechula* ("Butterfly"). She smiled wider and wider as the ride went on that day. Never had she felt so sure of herself. God was showering down his favor; she believed that wholeheartedly.

The day before the race, Spupaleena rode back down to the village. Pekam caught sight of her and jumped to his feet. He dropped his traps and ran toward his sister. Skumhist, however, gathered his traps and strode off in the opposite direction. Her heart sank as she watched his back vanish around the corner of his pit home. He refused to simply greet her.

She dismounted and handed Pekam the lead as they embraced.

"He's strong," she said with conviction.

"He looks it. His eyes are alert, and his whole body is solid. You have been working hard." Pekam stroked the gelding's body slowly with searching hands. "He's stout, but is he fast? Can he last and hold strong to the end without losing his wind?"

"Kewa, sintahoos, kewa." Spupaleena's eyes darted from shoulder to hindquarters, nodding in approval. She chuckled at the thought of the foolish boy's loss, only her fortunate gain.

Her gaze dropped as the image of her father's back flashed in her mind.

"He'll come around," Pekam said. Spupaleena looked up in surprise. "I've been talking to him. He's just afraid he'll lose you again. You need to assure him you won't ever run off like you did. He'll be okay. He's thinking of coming to watch you ride tomorrow."

"Loot, how did you?" A smile crossed her face and her eyes sparkled with glee.

"I convinced him this is the only way you'll be happy and that he needs to support you and let you be a woman, not a little girl."

"You amaze me, Pekam. Lim lumt. I owe you." She hugged her brother tightly.

"Yeah, we'll see if he comes first. Just give him time. Talk to him."

Spupaleena stared at the colt for a bit. "I can't talk to him; he won't listen." She took hold of her braids.

"Give him another chance; you might have to give him several chances."

"How did you get to be so smart for only eleven?" She winked.

Pekam chuckled as his face and neck grew flush. He chewed his lip. "I had to grow up fast when you left.

Mistum had a hard time; we all did." His voice grew thick with emotion.

Spupaleena suddenly felt shame encompass her. "I know. I'll try too." She pressed her hands together as if in prayer.

"If your God is real, won't he help?"

Spupaleena lifted her gaze to him. "Huh? You speak of God," she teased, holding her palms up in front of her.

Pekam's face reddened. "Kewa, I've been thinking. You've come back a different person—stronger and confident. Your thoughts are sharper. You don't just dream around all day." Pekam waved the flies away from his face.

They stood in silence for a brief moment. Spupaleena could merely smile and thank God silently. She had been praying for her family for three years—four counting the one she spent with the Gardners.

"Don't get excited, I'm just thinking," he added.

It was all she could do not to jump and dance around with delight. *I'll be praying for you some more, sintahoos,* she told herself. Inside, she was smiling as big and bright as the summer sun. Pekam pushed Spupaleena aside. "Let's get him put away. Besides, Rainbow's lonely."

She felt a flicker of hope for her brother and would start praying God's Word of salvation over him. It seemed his heart was softening; maybe he would finally let God in and soon.

Chapter 4

The starting cry echoed through the valley as the racers kicked their horses into motion. Hooves pounded, and hearts sped. Nee Ap Ḵukneeya reared up, nearly tossing his rider to the ground. Spupaleena did her best to rein him in as he spun in circles, wide-eyed. She reached back and let the end of her whip pop the colt's rump. The gelding lunged forward and took off down the straightaway, zigzagging as he caught his footing. Spupaleena hung off the side of her saddle. A few hops into the race, and she was able to right herself.

Disbelief crossed her face. She slapped the colt's rump several times, and he darted from one side of the crowd to the other, barely missing onlookers. He meandered all over the place as if he had been stung by a hornet. After several yards of hopping about, the horse finally gathered his senses and held steady, but it was too late. The others were far enough ahead, and there was no way they could gain enough momentum to catch up.

Crossing the finish line last, Spupaleena felt like running off and never showing her face in public again. Shame filled her every breath. She hung her head as she cooled off the gelding. The tables had turned, and she suddenly felt like the foolish boy. The crowd murmured their bewilderment. Spupaleena could hear the women ask one another how she could have lost. Astonishment filled the air, and it was a pungent odor.

By the time Pekam caught up to his sister, she was struggling to hold her tears in check. Her face was crossed with anguish, but her pride would not allow anyone to see her cry.

"Let's get home," Spupaleena said as she choked back the lump in her throat.

"What happened out there?"

"I don't know. He was ready—you saw him. I just don't understand, and right now, don't care." She felt defeated and perhaps a little bit humbled. She wiped her burning, sweat-soaked hands on her doeskin dress.

The two walked side by side in silence. Pekam knew better than to badger her for answers. He figured in time they could hash it all out. For now he would just help his sister put the gelding away and keep his mouth shut. *The ride back to the village will give her plenty of time to figure things out,* he thought. The warm evening breeze would cool everyone down. Things would surely look better in the morning.

"Now, stumpkeelt, maybe you will see the truth in my words." Skumhist rubbed his mixture of brain matter and water into a mule deer hide. "It's time you stop acting like a reckless boy." The muscles in his jaw clinched. He looked up at his daughter, expecting even a simple reply. Nothing.

Skumhist continued to rub the hides down with the animal brains. He had a few hides to finish and wanted the work to be complete by nightfall. There was much to be done, and he knew his spirited daughter thought she had better things to do and would be of no help. It would be hard enough to get his son to tan a hide now that his sister drew his attention to the worthless beasts.

Spupaleena just stood there. She decided long ago to never again raise her voice to her father. She respected him more than that even if they did fail to see eye to eye.

"Perhaps the loss of this race is the Creator's way of telling you it's over." Skumhist worked as he talked. "You don't wish to hear my words, but that is what I believe. It saddens me to see you hurt." He stopped, sighed, and looked up at her with sincere eyes.

"I know, mistum, but I believe God wants me to learn from this loss. My head was too big. I'll work harder and smarter this time. I will train with others, not just by myself. It was my fault. I trained alone, and the colt was threatened by the other horses."

"Loot, Spupaleena, it must end now before you get injured." He dipped his fingers in more of the slimy concoction and continued to work in small circles, softening his hide. "I keep telling you this. You refuse to listen, and you are blinded by your own desires. "Please, listen, if not for me, for your stimteema and your—"

"What? I ride for her and for Hamis-hamis," Spupaleena said, throwing her arms into the air. "I ride to honor them." She thrust a finger in the air, jabbing at nothing but her anger.

"To honor them?" Skumhist stood tall, shaking the dripping brains from his hands. "How is this honoring the dead?"

"I ride in their memory," she answered in a low, sturdy voice. She would not back down. She fought back the tears welling in her eyes. Her frustration made her feel like she would burst at any minute.

"Are you sure? How does neglecting one's duty to help the family ever honor anyone?"

Spupaleena had all she could take. She turned and sprinted off before she regretted what was to come out of her mouth. She was mortified. How could her father fathom her betraying her beloved grandmother? She ran until she reached a secluded fern patch hidden in a protective hedge of brush and fir trees just up the hill from the village. She hid in her favorite spot, allowing hot tears to stream from her swollen eyes. The coolness of the ferns surrounded her like a nice morning mist.

"I'm not lazy. Father God…" She plopped to the ground and pressed her face into the palms of her hands. "I know and believe you put this dream into my heart—help mistum see it too. Please give me a heart of courage. Lead me with your strong arms in the right direction. I'm hungry for your wisdom, Father, please lead me."

Spupaleena wept in the quietness of God's creation. It wasn't long before she was reminded that pity was not the answer, not even an option. She felt the Holy Spirit embrace her with faith and courage.

The following morning, Spupaleena packed the colt with a few necessities and crept out. The sun peeked its salmon-colored face over the mountains. She led the colt out of the village, careful to not step on too many dried leaves or tiny twigs. She craned her neck, making sure there were no followers, especially Pekam. He needed to stay behind and help their father. They would soon be moving camp to the Kettle Falls to trade with the sooyapee. This was the last push to have everything ready. She believed the work would be done in time without her help. *Mistum just won't let me go*, she thought. *He talks of me growing up, but he also fears it.* She shook her head as she imagined the look on his face the previous day. *He will see in time.*

Once she was certain no one was sneaking behind them and she was out of earshot, Spupaleena hoisted herself up into the saddle and urged the colt into a nice, steady trot. She was anxious to get him bareback—the only way they could float as one. Even though her saddle shadowed the feeling of his body movements, and the rocking motion was the same, the touch was different. Riding bareback felt personal and offered a special connection.

Spupaleena made her way to the Columbia River. Upon reaching her place to cross, she discovered several downed trees blocking the path. It looked as if the beavers had moved in and were making additions. She hopped off Nee Ap K<u>uk</u>neeya and dropped the reins, assuming he would ground–tie. As she reached for the first log to drag away, something spooked a nearby flock of turkeys, and they headed straight for the colt. He whinnied and loped off into the adjacent woods.

Off balance, she tripped, and her face landed in the mud. Spupaleena stood and kicked debris on the ground, watching it scatter. She let loose a rush of Native words as if the horse was supposed to know their meaning. Mud covered her almost from head to toe. She did her best to wipe it off, short of dunking herself in the frigid river, which might have been a better idea. It would have cooled her fiery temper.

"I thought I won a good horse." She set her hands on her hips. "I can't believe this." She shook her head. Cocking an ear, she searched the terrain, listening carefully for a crackle of broken branches or rustling of leaves the gelding might make. She heard nothing, only the chickadee's chirping like they were laughing at her.

Heat ran up her neck and spiked her forehead with beads of sweat. She strode back to the river to splash cool water on her face. She knew following after a horse only made them run away faster. It was a game to them—a game she was unwilling to play. *He'll be back*, she thought.

"Well, I'll just move your logs, and you'll have to either move your home or start over," she said to the hidden beaver family. She couldn't see them, but knew they were nearby.

Spupaleena set to work, dragging fallen log after fallen log off to the side. She grabbed branches and tossed them out of the path as well. Once a trail was wide enough to walk through, she washed her hands in the clear, flowing river. She then found a soft spot on some grass and lay on her back to rest for a bit. It wasn't long before she heard the rustle of leaves. She twisted over and leaned on her elbows, peering over her shoulder, snickering. There he was, Mr. Curious.

He was stepping out of the trees and into view, poking his nose at the ground. He sniffed the cool breeze and snorted. Eventually, he took a step toward Spupaleena. She dropped her gaze from his eye to his shoulder, taking the pressure off him. She also tilted her chin down like she was ignoring him. He took a couple more steps toward her. He nosed the grass, tasting its freshness.

They were still several yards apart. Spupaleena decided to stand and entice him over to her direction. She was willing to take every opportunity to get closer to him, giving him another chance to correct his mistakes and overcome his fears. He needed to hook back on to her; trust her to protect him.

She kept her gaze on his shoulder, the opposite of what a predator would do. She was beckoning his friendship, not stalking him for her next meal. She continued to drift toward him, walking side to side and holding the back of her hand out for him to sniff. She slumped her shoulders and kept her gaze down to the ground.

The colt took a step in her direction, keeping his eyes locked on her. He began to shift his hind end from left to right, facing her as if they were partners dancing on the beach. He mirrored her movements as she reeled him in, lowering his head and licking his lips as he began to respect her leadership. It was not long until she had her hands on his neck, rubbing him and rewarding his connection.

To his surprise, she took a step away. He lowered his head, still licking, and followed her lead. "Yeah, you're a good boy," she whispered, stroking his neck. She gathered the reins and stuck her foot into the stirrup, raising herself into the saddle. She softly waved her feet, encouraging the colt to walk on. She appreciated the gelding's willingness to please her. They crossed the belly-deep river and scrambled up the bank to the other side. She urged him into a trot, using fallen logs and brush, bending his body from left to right, softening his neck and strengthening his lungs. She had learned in the last few years that a busy colt was a safe colt.

Like anyone, horses need a job. When their minds were engaged, so was their heart. In the past her daydreaming only left her on the ground eating dust. She would only make that mistake once. She took advantage of the trail to the Gardners, which was filled with fun obstacles; it also made the time go by quickly. She could never imagine living like the plains people, no mountains to climb nor trees to shade and circle. How boring it would be to ride through a burning-hot, mindless prairie.

Spupaleena was sitting at the table with Delbert on her lap. She bobbed her knees up and down, giving him a wild pony ride. He howled as his cheeks jiggled in rhythm to the motion. He could hardly contain his little boy laughter. After awhile, she was worn out, her arms having a good workout. She passed him off to Elizabeth and took a sip of her mint tea, breathing in the smoothness.

She studied him on his mother's lap, amused at his baldness. Kids from her village usually had a head full of coal-black hair. Delbert had a mere dusting of reddish-blonde fluff. He looked like a little, old man. He was such a darling little toddler, and she loved to run her fingers over his fuzzy head.

"Delbert is so *sweenompt* ("Handsome")." Spupaleena clucked at him, and he gave her a charming grin in return. The toddler twisted himself out of his mother's lap and padded over to his daddy. Elizabeth felt relieved to have a break. Phillip held out his long arms and scooped his son on to his lap, taking over where Spupaleena left off. He now had one squealing rider on each knee. Hannah giggled and leaned over, trying to tickle her brother.

There was a knock on the door, and Jack Dalley walked in. His six-foot-two stocky frame blocked most of the afternoon light trying to peer around him. Jack's and Phillip's gazes locked momentarily. They smiled and looked elsewhere.

"Hello, everyone," he said, blustering through the door. He hung his Stetson on a peg and strode over to the table where everyone sat. Phillip pulled a chair over for him and he plopped down.

"Howdy, neighbor," Phillip replied, snuffing out his excitement.

"Hi, Jack," the ladies said in unison. They looked at each other and giggled.

Hannah wiggled out of her daddy's lap and hopped over to Jack, wrapping her chubby, little arms around his leg. "Uncle Jack!" He bent over and gathered her up in his burly arms and showered her with kisses. She giggled at his attention.

"It's good to see you, Jack." Spupaleena stood, extending her hand in greeting.

"You too. How are things with your family? How's your father?" He put a free arm around her shoulder, giving her a slight squeeze. She dropped her arm and briefly leaned into his hug. Delbert bumped into her as he made his way back to his mother.

Her face glowed red. "They're good, busy tanning the last of the hides for trade." He nodded, understanding the hard work involved. "Are either of you able to trade any goods this year?" she asked.

Jack glanced at Phillip, stifling a laugh. He shook his head. Spupaleena looked at Elizabeth, who was smiling like a little girl with a secret.

"Spup." Phillip rubbed his hands together. He no longer could hold in his bubbling enthusiasm.

"What?" She looked at each person around the table. They all dropped their gazes to the floor, smiling brightly. "What's going on? You're all acting like a bunch of little kids who took an extra treat behind your mother's back." She chuckled, finished off her tea, and held the cup in her lap. "You're all crazy," she added, setting her cup on the table. She grabbed her braids and slid her hands down to the ends, holding on tightly.

Everyone did their best to smother the amusement. Spupaleena's eyes flitted from person to person as the color rising from her neck burned bright. Her gaze landed on Delbert, who was getting mighty squirrely in his mother's lap. He looked like his grandpa, Phillip's dad, and the boy's namesake. Both were short and stocky. Both were spitfires.

The suspense finally overtook Phillip. "Okay, my friend, we have a surprise for you."

Spupaleena shot her attention to him. She flashed him a quizzical look and put her palms up into the air. "What?" She wondered what could be so darn comical—a practical joke? *I better brace myself,* she thought. Anything was possible with those two men.

"Come on, follow us." Jack motioned everyone up and led the way to the barn. Spupaleena suspiciously and cautiously lagged behind. She fingered the fringe on her dress. Her nervousness took her by surprise. All the sudden her mouth went dry and she broke out in a sweat. She wondered why she was reacting this way. She was somewhat embarrassed.

Sammy nickered his greeting as the group approached the corral. Once they were at the gate, he was nosing for his treat. Spupaleena opened her fist, letting the Paint nibble a carrot out of her open hand.

She pressed her face against his soft coat. She recalled their first meeting, his soft winter hair, and big, marbled eyes. She fell in love that instant and knew her life would always include horses.

Chapter 5

Phillip pulled a handkerchief out of his back pocket and tied it behind Spupaleena's head. Now she really could feel her heart race. She was sure everyone could clearly hear the pounding.

"No peeking," he teased. She felt for the wooden rail and held on. A shiver ran across her back. Elizabeth quietly walked up behind her and placed a hand on her shoulder. Spupaleena could feel her friend's warm breath on the back of her neck. Then she felt Elizabeth hold it in and softly gasp. Something special was about to happen, not any silly joke.

Jack led the Tobiano stud out and in front of everyone. Spupaleena trembled as she heard the clip-clop of each hoof as it hit the ground. Once the colt was in place, Elizabeth slowly lifted the bandana off Spupaleena's eyes. She gasped loudly, nearly choking, reaching for his soft muzzle with her shaking hands.

Her gaze traveled the length of the muscular sixteen-two-hand horse.

He was mostly black with what looked like a white lightning bolt running the length of his left shoulder and spilling down his leg. He also had a white bear claw looking form painted over his rump. All four legs were white with big, strong hooves and a white blaze snaking down his nose. He had large, soft, ebony eyes that communicated gentleness. He sniffed her hands as tears rolled down her face and pooled in her cupped palms.

The colt looked at her as if saying everything would be just fine and they would surely make a good team. Spupaleena quivered like a young girl seeing the mighty Kettle Falls for the first time. She was so full of sentiment that no words entered into her mind, only emotions and pictures that left as quickly as they came. She merely soaked in God's blessing.

"He's yours, sister," Elizabeth whispered as she hugged the girl from behind. Spupaleena let the stud nibble her hands; she could only nod. She was amazed how well-behaved he was, standing as still and quiet as a well-trained dog.

She looked at Jack and Phillip with watery eyes and nodded. She struggled to get past the lump in her throat. Elizabeth stepped back, allowing Spupaleena room to walk around the amazing creature. But, she just stood there, unable to move. Her legs felt weak. Phillip, Jack, and Elizabeth all looked at one another and smiled. They had never seen their friend this stunned.

Phillip handed her the lead rope. "Why don't you take him for a walk?"

Her arms remained at her sides. "Why…" She shook her head, willing herself to hold back more tears.

"Spup, you need a horse that has as much heart as you have." Phillip limped over and put his arm around her shoulder. She looked at him, numb and thoughtless.

Jack stood on the other side of her, his broad hand leaning on the other one. "I bred him especially for you. I've started him, but it's up to you to do the rest. We will work with you to fine tune him—"

"How will I ever repay you?" She turned to Jack. "I'll sell Rainbow's colts and pay you back." She nodded her head in determination. She would never take handouts; it was against her family's way.

The men laughed, and Phillip drew her closer. "My friend, he's a gift. The only payment you need is to ride him with all your heart and dedication." He again held out the lead rope to her.

"But—"

"But nothing, my little sister. Make us proud. He's the beginning of a great line for you. I know your father is against this way of life, but there are many successful ranchers, and you have what it takes to make it work. Skumhist will see that in time. Jack and I have done well. After I returned home from the…from Lincoln, with only one workable leg, I learned to ride again. We made it work." Phillip glanced at his wife, who nodded in support. "Now here, take him!" He shoved the lead rope into her hands and stepped back, as did Jack. Her fingers wrapped tightly around the rope as it sank in that the animal was really hers.

Spupaleena stood, staring at the colt. "I know you mean well. But, my mistum is so upset about my riding, I pray for him every day. I guess it'll take time, and I'll have to prove myself to him. Pekam told me mistum thinks he'll lose me again, but I've grown up. I could never leave my family." She reached up and stroked the colt's sleek neck. "But I don't know how to convince him this is what God is leading me to do—my path in life."

Phillip nodded, understanding a father's protection for his daughter. "We'll help in any way we can. You can even bring him over, and we can show him the place and educate him in the business." He leaned against the corral, taking the weight off his amputated limb.

"We'll also pray for him," Elizabeth added.

"We can show him the cattle and how our life has actually become simpler. We do have to harvest more hay for the winter months, but we can also show him the benefits of working the colts on cattle," Jack said enthusiastically. He took his hat off and in a playful manner, twirled it around and slapped it back on his wavy black head.

"He's more than welcome to travel over here and see for himself," Elizabeth interjected.

Spupaleena raised her eyebrows. She was getting her wit back and her body started to relax. "Playing with cows? What are you talking about?" She shrugged her shoulders. She had never heard of horses playing with cows. The idea was absurd, but with Jack and Phillip, anything was possible; they were crazy enough to make it happen.

"We'll show you tomorrow." Jack flashed her an enormous grin, his eyes dancing in the afternoon sun. He suddenly felt like a teenage boy again.

Spupaleena stepped away from the men and walked around her new partner. Now that the shock of the surprise was over, she could see how beautiful and majestic he really was. His ears followed her every move. She let her hand sweep over the three-year-old's back. She studied his legs for straightness, his hindquarters for power, and his neck for strength and balance. He was the most striking animal she had ever seen. She hoped his mind and confidence matched his eye-catching confirmation.

"What's his name?" Spupaleena asked as she reached on her tiptoes and fingered his forelock.

"We came up with something good." The three friends looked at one another, smiling like children hiding a new puppy from their mother.

"Well?" She turned to face the men, with a not-so-sure-about-this look on her face. *This should be interesting*, she thought.

Phillip nodded to Jack. "Smok'n Dust," Jack announced as proud as a new parent.

Spupaleena threw her head back and laughed. "Smok'n Dust," she repeated. She thought for a minute about the funny long name. "I like it. How did you come up with that?"

Jack clapped his hands together, leaning slightly forward. "We figured the other horses will be eatin' his dust 'cause he'll be smok'n the ground with his speed—fast and powerful like the clap of thunder." The men beamed, obviously tickled with their choice of name. Spupaleena glanced at Elizabeth, opened mouthed, looking for some female support.

Elizabeth stood with a drowsy Delbert in her arms, stifling a laugh, not wanting to awaken his energy. Spupaleena eyed her, finally bursting out as they all laughed aloud. Elizabeth had to walk away with the baby so he would fall asleep.

This was the second best day of her life, the first being her reunion with her father three years back. Her coal eyes beamed in the afternoon sun and she stood somewhat taller, tossing her braids behind her.

"Now take him on a walk. Tomorrow, the fun begins," Phillip said, tapping his walking stick on his wooden leg.

Spupaleena turned and led the colt down the trail that led toward Jack's place. "Smok'n Dust." She shook her head, still chuckling. "Let's get acquainted, shall we?" He whinnied as if to agree, his head towering over her a good foot.

Pekam stretched, ready for the day's ride. He was jumping up and down by the fire in his tule-pit home, partly from anticipation and partly to wake up his sleepy body. "What will we do, where will we ride?" He reached for his moccasins and laced them up. Darting out the flap door, he scurried over to Spupaleena's place, sucking in the cool, moist air. It was a bright morning that felt as fresh as a cool, clear, rushing creek.

"Spupaleena," he hollered. There was no answer. "<u>Lth</u>kickha, time to get up. Come on, little racing rabbit, time to circle the trees, jump the logs, and cross the streams," he teased. He slapped his hands together, feeling like he would burst.

Still no answer.

"I'm comin' in…"

To his surprise, the dwelling was empty. He looked around; her elk robe was gone as were her teas and herbs. He searched the room frantically. His heart sank, and he could feel the color drain from his face.

"Loot!" he shouted, making a fist in the air. Pekam turned and sprinted out the door. He ran as fast as his legs would carry him to the corral where Rainbow stood soaking in the morning sun. She whinnied, ready to be tethered outside and munch on the rich, green grass. He kicked the dirt and punched one of the wooden rails encircling the waiting mare. "Loot," he cried. "Why did you leave me behind?" he screeched. He fell to his knees, anger twisting his face. "I'm tired of being left behind. How can I keep learning?" He shook his head. There was an empty pit in his stomach.

After a short moment, he stood and haltered Rainbow, staked her out, and went in search of his father. He knew how Skumhist would react and dreaded telling him the news. Seeing his father resting outdoors by the fire, he braced himself, drew in a deep breath, and walked forward.

"No, bring your hand out to the side and gently draw his head toward your hip," Jack said in a calm and gentle voice. "When you feel the rein slacken, let go like it's on fire and burning your hand off." He smiled at Spupaleena. She was progressing rapidly with her lessons.

"Like this?" She was trying to get her feel and timing of the colt's response to her hands just right.

"Yeah, but you need to slow your hands down. You're jerking him in too quickly. Allow your fingers to be soft. Relax and breathe in deeply, letting it out slowly, and melt into him." Jack showed her exactly what he was looking for with his own bald-faced gelding. He took his burly hands and clutched a rein, bending his mount to the left. As soon as the horse put his nose in toward his side, Jack let go of the rein, simply tossing it forward. He made it all seem so simple. His timing was flawless.

Spupaleena had never ridden this tall or powerful of a horse. She needed to capture more of his attention and trust. His mind was still focused a tad too much on his surroundings. With this large of a horse, she needed all of his concentration on her slightest movement. Once she had that, his body would follow. She had quickly learned that these soft and kind methods offered trust and willingness, which she would need every ounce of come race day.

Jack had shown her what it was to dance with a horse over the past few years. She and Dusty were well on their way. That was her goal—to dance.

Spupaleena bent the colt around rocks and trees, and he was becoming softer and softer to where she only needed a couple fingers to tenderly guide him at any speed. She could feel his neck come around freely. He refused to fight her in any way.

"Kewa, his whole body seems relaxed. I feel like I have more control over him. He's so strong." She reined Dusty to a halt, allowing him to catch his breath.

"He is, but you can handle him, Spup, I know he will work well for you." Jack nodded, his expression full of pride as if she was his own daughter. "Keep bending him on both sides; we need those ribs soft as a kitten. When you're done, we'll go for a ride, and remember, if he tries to get away from you, catch it early and bend that big head of his around, using your legs as well, and his back end will follow. We'll start slow and gradually add speed." Jack took his Stetson off and rustled his hair. "Oh, and don't pull back with both hands; he's not ready for that yet." He patted his cowboy hat back on his head and watched Spupaleena some more, ready to fire advice her way as needed.

"Kewa, I agree. Where are we going, anyway?" She looked around, searching for the possible direction.

Jack chuckled. "It's a surprise, remember?" He had some cattle get away from him in a rocky valley nearby; he was aware it would be a stretch for Dusty but knew without a shadow of a doubt that Spupaleena would bring him through it. He only dreamed of having a portion of her talent.

He loved to watch her ride. She was so graceful on horseback, as a whitetail deer running through the forest, smooth and bold.

Skumhist looked up from his morning fire. He was sipping the last of his tea before starting the final preparations for the annual excursion north to the Great Falls. His pelts and hides were ready by the canoe and just needed to be loaded. This year, he would paddle up river and was excited for the new adventure. In years past, the pelts had been carried on backpacks with the help of his family members. Skumhist was making mental notes of last-minute tasks that still remained. He needed yet to make final inspections of his nets for salmon fishing. He looked forward to getting his hands on the glorious creatures. Nothing made him feel more like a man than hauling a ninety-pound salmon up a steep bank. His body trembled at the thought.

His muscles were sore from the previous day's work of packing each item in its rightful place. He was getting older and tired easily but would never admit it. He noticed his son coming toward him. Pekam had shot up in the last couple of months. He was tall and lean yet still awkward in his eleven-year-old frame. His disheveled braids were flopping behind him as he strode up to his father.

"She's gone…again," he bellowed, waving his hands above his head.

Skumhist glanced up from the fire and into his son's angry eyes. "Where is she this time?" Pekam sat by his father and then quickly stood again.

"Who knows? The colt's gone too." Rage enveloped Pekam. He peered down at his father, who just sat there, looking sad and whipped. "What are we going to do?" he persisted. The boy paced in front of his father. He stopped, picked up a fist full of dirt, and threw it into the bushes.

Skumhist drew his attention back to the orange coals of the dying fire. He shrugged his shoulders. "What can we do? She has a mind of her own. She's a free spirit—always has been." He rubbed his forehead. He had long since given up trying to corral his daughter. She would allow herself to be tethered as much as the young stallion she rode. They were an exact pair.

Pekam turned to his father. "Do you think her God—Jesus, as she says—put it in her to race?"

Skumhist shook his head, staring into the fire. "Loot! She has always been a dreamer; she makes her reality fit her fantasies. I hope this is a short-lived rabbit trail. When she tires of her little games, she'll settle down and live like a woman should." He peered in his cup and tossed the remaining water into the fire. The flames hissed and a small tendril of smoke curled up into the air.

Pekam snickered, slapping his leg. "Mistum, she's never been a woman."

Skumhist looked at his son; his eyes softened, and he laughed. "You're right, I guess I shouldn't have allowed her to trap with me so much and made her learn the ways of her stimteema."

Pekam laughed and then grew serious. "When will she return?"

"Soon. She always comes back within a few weeks. You'll see." Skumhist sat calmly with his elbows on his knees. He was finished fighting with his daughter. Perhaps she was right, he needed to let her live her own life; make her own decisions.

Pekam nodded. *I hope so,* he thought. He hated to be without his sister. He hated to ride alone, and he hated tanning hides with his father. He loved time spent with Skumhist; he'd just rather be out traipsing around the mountains on a horse, any horse. He and Rainbow were becoming good friends, and she was forever testing his riding abilities. He wished his family could raise horses and quit trapping. Would his father ever agree?

Skumhist finally got up and went to complete last minute tasks before heading out. After equipment was inspected and the canoe was loaded, Skumhist, Pekam, and a cousin shoved off from the riverbank and paddled up river. Skumhist's heart was heavy leaving without his daughter. Nevertheless, he would not let her antics ruin his time at the falls. He relished the time spent with other tribes and his white trapper friends. He fixed his eyes on the terrain ahead of him and paddled with quick and even strokes. No matter what, this was going to be a glorious day.

Chapter 6

Spupaleena beamed as she and Dusty traversed the country in rhythm. She felt they were connecting like horse and rider should with trust and confidence.

"We're almost there," Jack hollered over at Spupaleena. Jack reined in his gelding. Spupaleena took her cue, and she circled the colt around. As his feet slowed, she melted into her saddle, slowly and quietly as Dusty came to a smooth stop like a duck on a pond.

"He's looking much better," Phillip said. Jack had rigged up a special stirrup to secure Phillip's wooden leg. Although he no longer trapped, Sammy offered him a way to get around, and he was able to keep up with the other men. Jack eventually offered him a partnership in the cattle business, knowing he needed help and support. The pair made great business partners. Jack worked mostly with the colts and bringing in the hay, while Phillip tended the cows and repaired the fence lines.

At first, Phillip was unsure if he could handle the demands, but after days of prayer and Jack's modified saddle, he quickly came on board. He has never looked back since. Phillip was thankful he had his wife's support. She had told him he needed to do what made him happy—something he could live with and love to do. She was such an encouragement; Phillip knew long ago he married the perfect woman.

Spupaleena flashed him a sassy smile; she felt like she could beat anyone who came against her, whether spiritual or in her world of racing. She knew spiritual battles all too well and no longer feared them. She knew the power of the name of Jesus and was learning when to call on him.

She was confident.

The colt was ready.

Her focus was on God.

Now, she just needed a race.

"Kewa, he feels like he is floating on a trail of clouds." Phillip slapped his leg, and all three laughed until their bellies ached. The girl's joy never grew old toward the two men. They found inspiration in her youthful, courageous spirit.

They all quickly grew serious as the brush behind them rattled and their horses snorted and shot their ears forward. Sammy whirled in circles and danced, pawing the ground viciously. The humans struggled to make out what was hiding in the brush, but the horses knew. They could smell it, and the aroma screamed danger.

Phillip heard a shriek and saw Spupaleena's stud colt spin and gallop off out of the corner of his eye, as if a lightning strike caught Dusty in the rump. Jack's gelding reared up in time to nick a cougar in the face in midair with his front hooves. Time seemed to stop as Phillip watched wide-eyed. He pulled out his Colt .45 and shot in the air. Sammy turned and twisted, making it impossible to aim for the cougar.

Fortunately, the piercing boom of the pistol was enough to scare the predator off. He leapt up onto a boulder and tore off into the woods.

"Where's Spup?" Jack asked as he reeled Copper, his ten-year-old gelding, around, searching intently for any sign of the girl. He was grateful to be riding this sure-footed mount that had speed and the mind of a well seasoned cow horse.

"They ran off that way." Phillip pointed east.

"Oh, no, Lord, help her. Come on, she's headed toward a gnarly drop-off," Jack said as he kicked his gelding into a gallop.

Phillip never thought twice about his wooden leg. He followed close behind. His balance was solid, and he had ridden enough years that staying seated was second nature.

"Whoa!" Spupaleena shouted. She doubted the colt could hear over his pounding hoof beats. She was clearly seated on a runaway horse. Dusty was not contemplating a slower gait. He ran like he was in the race of his life; in fact, he was gaining speed. The colt was wide-eyed with nostrils flaring. His lungs sounded like they would burst at any moment. Dust billowed from the trail behind them.

Spupaleena tried to bend the stud colt around, pulling with all her might, but he had his nose pointed forward and was not about to change course. He was running to save his life. He had only one thing on his mind—*run!* His neck was stiff and straight, and sweat ran down his chest and legs. Spupaleena had no idea how she was going to stop this powerful freight train. She figured he would eventually tire and want to slow down by himself—but when? She would just have to let him run it out for now.

The most critical issue that faced her at the moment was her lack of familiarity of the country they were quickly eating up. Spupaleena was growing nervous but knew better than to let Dusty catch wind of it. She would have to remain as calm as possible. Looking around, the horizon seemed to have a long wide gap in it. Before she could react, the stallion hurled over a fallen larch tree and plummeted down a ravine. Spupaleena found herself airborne, landing with a thud on the side of a hill. She tumbled down to the bottom and came to a halt in a bed of rocks.

Dusty managed to land on all fours and sprinted away. Spupaleena could hear the hoof beats growing faint. She tried to look around, but all was a blur. She pressed her head into her forearm as she lay on her stomach, praying Phillip and Jack would find her. She hoped they would figure out which direction she had sped off. Then in a flash, all went dark.

It wasn't long before the men rode up on her motionless form. Dusty left an obvious trail of deepened hoof prints along with broken, scattered debris.

"Spupaleena," Jack said as he jumped off his still-moving mount. He ran to her lifeless body and kneeled by her side. Fear crossed his face. "Spup, talk to me." His body shook, and he could hardly take in a breath; his chest felt like it would cave in.

He gently shook her.

There was no response.

Phillip reined in Sammy, heaved his leg out of the stirrup, and jumped out of the saddle. As the wooden surrogate hit the ground, it gave out and he rolled on the ground. Phillip turned onto his stomach and crawled the rest of the way over to his friend's side. "No, not again," he said, shaking his head. Tears pooled in his eyes. "I can't lose her, not this time." He looked at Jack. "We have to get her to Elizabeth." Jack nodded and the men instinctively laid their hands on the girl and prayed healing over her. They also prayed for a safe return back to the cabin.

Jack took notice of her waist-long hair, which was sprawled out in all directions. Before they left her braids were tightly woven, as usual. This puzzled him because those braids were tied off securely. *How fast was the colt traveling? How fast did she tumble down this ravine?* he wondered. He ran his fingers through his hair, trembling. "Oh, my Lord," was all he could mutter.

"She must have been tossed pretty hard," Phillip said. Jack nodded; he was too choked up to speak.

Carmen Peone

Phillip glanced over at Jack, who was as white as fresh snow. "This isn't your fault," he said.

"Isn't it?" He torn his Stetson off his head and threw it to the ground.

"No, we both know she can handle him. This could have happened to any one of us."

Jack just stared at the broken, limp figure lying in front of him.

Phillip leaned in close to his friend. "Spup, stay with us," he whispered.

She moaned and wiggled her fingers. The guys looked at each other with astonished grins; their eyes round and relieved. Phillip picked up her petite, scuffed-up hand and held it in his like a father to a daughter.

"Spup, we're here…we'll get you back, just hold on." Jack wiped a tear from his cheek.

"Kewa…" Spupaleena could barely muster the energy to form the word.

"Thank you, Lord," Phillip whispered, closing his eyes briefly. He grabbed his stub leg as a sharp pain shot though like a bullet. He held his breath until it eased.

"You okay?" Jack asked.

"Ya." Phillip winced. "Let's just get her out of here. I just landed wrong; I'll live…"

"My head hurts," Spupaleena moaned. She choked, then rolled over and threw up. She lay on her side, willing her mind to quit spinning.

"Do you think you broke anything?" Jack asked.

"Loot, I just feel like I've been in a fight with a rock and lost." The men chuckled, happy she was talking.

"I think you're right," Phillip said. He gently examined her arm, ribs, and legs. Nothing seemed broken.

"Just lay still until you think you can be moved," Jack added. "I think you just got the wind knocked out of you is all."

"Okay, where's Dusty?" Spupaleena moaned. Her face hurt. Her legs hurt. Everything hurt. Her lungs burned with every breath.

"Don't worry… " Phillip struggled to tell her.

"Is he okay?" Spupaleena slurred.

The guys glanced at one another, not sure if they should tell her or not. Phillip finally answered. "He's not here. He ran off, but he must be all right. I would think if he was hurt, he'd be close by and we'd be able to hear him."

Jack scanned the area then replied. "I'll look for him later. He can't be far."

Spupaleena let out a pitiful chuckle. "Do you know how fast he was going?" She pressed a hand against her forehead.

"How fast?" Phillip winked at Jack.

"Like a flash of light. I've never been on a horse that traveled that fast. We need to teach him to stop," Spupaleena coughed. The pain in her sides and head made her wince and curl into a ball.

Elizabeth dropped her hoe as she saw Jack leading Spupaleena on the back of his horse, keeping one hand on the lead and one hand supporting the girl. She stood, gathered her skirt, and ran to them. Memories and heartache from her previous incident filled her soul.

"What happened?" she sputtered, reaching them in a matter of seconds.

"A cougar caught us off guard, and the colt bolted," Phillip said.

"Oh, Lord, no!" Elizabeth drew her hand over her mouth. She searched her friend for visible wounds. "How bad are you hurt?"

"I think she has another concussion, but nothing's broke. She's pretty bruised but should heal good enough," Jack answered for her.

"I'll be okay. I have a horrible headache, but I'm counting on you to work your magic, sister." Spupaleena held a hand up to her head, giving Elizabeth a sloppy grin.

"Glad you still have a sense of humor," Elizabeth said, smiling yet still concerned. "Let's get you down and into bed. I'll let you boys handle that, but be careful." Elizabeth turned on her heels and hurried into the cabin.

Jack peered at his friend's profile. He stared as Phillip watched his wife scurry away. She could do nor say anything wrong; one could see the trust and love in his eyes.

Jack snorted. "Come on, brother. Let's do as the boss orders." He waved Phillip over.

"Yeah, yeah, I'm com'n." Phillip turned his attention to Sammy and stroked his nose, hobbling toward Jack.

"You sure you're okay?"

"Ya, just bruised the nub is all. No bronc rid'n for me any time soon."

Jack laughed and slapped his partner on the back.

Spupaleena managed to smile through her pain, knowing Jack hit the nail square on.

Elizabeth darted about the cabin, gathering her herbs and bandages, humming as she worked. She was thankful Delbert and Hannah were napping, which would allow her to attend to Spupaleena without interruptions.

"Lay her on my bed," Elizabeth said, waving her hand to hurry the men along. They gently placed her on the bed and then left to tend to the horses and make a plan to track down the colt.

"This should be easy compared to the first time we met." Elizabeth smiled that loving and gentle way as she helped Spupaleena get comfortable.

"Kewa, I'm not nearly as broken," she said, her voice trailing off. She took in small, deliberate breaths to avoid the intense pain electrifying her body.

"You must have landed on a blanket of fluffy angels."

Spupaleena chuckled. "Except they forgot to slide one under my head."

Elizabeth laughed, shaking her head. She was impressed with Spupaleena's wittiness in the midst of such agony. Oh, how the girl had blossomed in just a few short years. Elizabeth was in high spirits to have her sister back for a time, just not like this.

"I'll go back and search for Dusty. I'm certain he's stopped by now, and more than likely, pretty frightened," Jack said, checking his cinch.

"Sounds good. I'll stay here and help my wife and rest my leg. It's starting to stiffen up on me." Phillip lifted his wooden leg and moved it in a front-to-back motion, attempting to loosen his muscles.

"Man, I haven't seen you ride like that since Sammy was a colt," Jack said jokingly.

Phillip slapped his partner on the back. "Yeah, since yesterday." He threw his head back and laughed heartily. The two could relax now that Spupaleena had been delivered safely. She was in, as Phillip put it, the hands of the most talented healer around the territory.

Jack mounted Copper and squeezed him into a trot. Not looking back, he waved his arm in the air. "Be back soon," he hollered.

"Be safe," Phillip replied.

Jack patted his bulging scabbard.

Phillip watched him ride off; a middle-aged, giant of a man with the presence of a teddy bear. His heart was as big as he was. If anyone could find the colt, Jack could. *No worries*, Phillip sighed. He pitched some hay to Sammy and headed for the cabin.

"He appears to be sound," Phillip said, rubbing his hands down one of Dusty's legs. "No heat anywhere."

"He never took a lame step the whole way home." Jack rubbed the colt's nose. "He was just around the bend when I found him, not but sixty yards away, standing in the shade of some aspen trees. His coat was dry, sweat caked but dry, and his eyes were calm." Jack continued his thorough examination of the colt.

"I would've figured he'd be spooked as young as he is." Phillip stood and leaned against the wall of the barn.

"Surprised me too." Jack rubbed his back, searching for soreness on his own body.

Phillip nodded. "He's solid, strong, fast. Do you think she can handle him?" Phillip asked, his eyes full of concern.

"Nah, she can control him. This was a good test of what still needs to be done, more work and time is all. We'll go slower and gradually add speed; she'll have to keep bending him and add rollbacks and do more with the cows, keep his brain busier. He'll do fine. Too many riders merely gallop their colts; adding all the other elements will make his mind mature, and he'll gain way more confidence, which is what he needs." Jack looked Phillip in the eye. "Once we get his mind, and I mean all of it, he'll respond to her slightest touch. Oh, he *will* be ready." Jack nodded, conviction in his tone.

The men watched the stud for a bit. "When is his next race?" Jack asked.

Phillip shook his head. "Not for a while, anyhow. She may just have to miss one or two. Better to be safe."

"I agree with that." Jack patted the stud on his rump. "But you get to tell her!"

"Thanks." Phillip rubbed his stub.

"Anytime partner." Jack winked.

"Well, I guess we can put him up and see what my wife has cookin'. I'm starved," Phillip said.

Jack smiled. He loved Elizabeth's cooking. Since his wife had passed away years ago, he was forced to eat his own miserable meals. "Count me in!"

Elizabeth sat in her rocker humming "I Surrender All". Spupaleena was tended to and resting. Elizabeth knew the children would wake up soon, so she stole this moment to close her eyes and simply be with God. She was all too thankful that her beloved friend was not seriously injured. Once was more than enough.

She thought back to the awful day they had met. Elizabeth had never seen a young girl in such bad shape. Blood and vomit matted her hair. Her face was bruised and cut. She looked over at Spupaleena who had been watching her.

"I have never told you this, but your voice is like the heavens. When you hum, I feel a peace and calm that floods my entire being." Spupaleena smiled.

"Thank you." Elizabeth could feel her face redden but was thrilled at the compliment. It meant a great deal coming from Spupaleena. "You hungry?"

"Kewa, very hungry," Spupaleena said softly. She was relaxed and feeling no pain after drinking the herbal tea Elizabeth made. Her eyes drooped, but the hunger overtook her will to sleep.

"Good, I'm glad your appetite's back."

"It's more than back. I feel like I could eat a whole pig."

Elizabeth laughed. "Interesting choice of words."

"Better than admitting to being one." Spupaleena giggled, waking up Hannah.

The child slid off her own little bed and padded over to Spupaleena and crawled up, snuggling under the quilt with her auntie. "Who's a pig?" The ladies snickered.

"No one. We're just saying how hungry we are," Spupaleena said.

"I'm hungry too." Hannah yawned, rubbing her eyes. "Will you fix my braids? They're fallin' out. They need to be like yours, Auntie Spuppy."

"Kewa, we'll fix them—"

"No, Hannah, you let your auntie rest. She's been hurt and needs to rest." Her mother flashed a look that told her she had better mind and not question anything. Hannah dropped her lower lip.

"Yes, Mamma," she whispered.

"We'll fix them in a few days when I feel better." Spupaleena grinned at the girl.

Hannah gently brushed her tiny fingers across Spupaleena's brown cheek. "I'm sorry you don't feel good."

"Aw, I'm okay, just need a couple days' rest and your mommy's good medicine, and I'll be up and riding again."

Hannah nestled up close to her auntie with as gentle movements as a four-year-old possibly could make. She pressed her little head into the crook of Spupaleena's neck and lay still. She took her pudgy little hand and placed it on her auntie's chest, patting it softly. "I love you, Auntie Spuppy," she whispered as her heavy eyes closed. "What happened to make you hurt?"

Spupaleena smiled, caressing Hannah's little arm. The little girl in this moment stole a piece of her heart that could never be taken back. Two hearts became locked together forever.

"I love you too." Spupaleena lay quiet in bed, soaking up the warmth the precious miniature body next to her radiated. She glanced down to see the little one fast asleep.

Elizabeth watched the two. A smile crossed her face as she was thankful her daughter had an auntie to spend time with. She poured herself a steaming cup of mint tea and sat down for a break. "I have a new verse for you; I think you'll like it." She wiped her hands on the floral apron and reached for her Bible.

"Yeah, I could use some new ones," Spupaleena said enthusiastically.

"Here it is, in the book of John. It reads, 'When the spirit of truth comes, he will guide you into all truth. He will not speak on his own but will tell you what he has heard. He will tell you about the future.'"

Spupaleena let the words sink in for a moment then replied, "Kewa, I like that. We need to follow God and his Word, not our own understanding, let alone someone else's. I keep trying to tell my mistum that, but he doesn't get it yet. Someday, I just keep praying for him. I don't know what else to do." She let out a frustrating sigh and stroked Hannah's silky hair.

"I know. It's comforting to know that God holds our future in his big, strong hands. We pray for your family all the time. Your father is an amazing man, full of love and determination." Elizabeth chuckled, *Like someone else I know.*

"But I still have to make the effort; we can't just wait around and expect good tidings to fall in our laps." Spupaleena only wished things were that easy.

"I agree; we also have to do things for the right reasons and with the attitude and heart that glorifies God and no one else."

Spupaleena fell silent. She knew her heart failed to line up with God's will, but she was reluctant to let go of her anger. She had a tight hold of rage and knew it was wrong, but right now, she could care less because it was that rage that kept her going. Rage kept her fighting for a way of life that would allow others to swim upstream instead of merely going with the flow of a meandering creek.

"Hello, ladies," Phillip said as the men entered the cabin. "Smells good."

The women quickly hushed them in unison. The guys looked over at Hannah and quietly hung their hats on the pegs by the door and tip-toed to sit at the table.

Elizabeth gave Spupaleena a look that said they would talk more later. She nodded and was relieved, not wanting to be bothered with her own prideful desires.

Chapter 7

The following morning, Phillip rode off at the break of day to round up the last of the wandering cattle. His nub was stiff, but the herbs his wife gave to him eased the soreness. Phillip admitted finding the strays would be easy, herding them back to the others would be the challenge. Jack would meet up with him, but having one of those herding dogs would be a bonus. A couple of good working dogs would make life that much simpler. He would bring that up to Jack after a bit of frustration got a hold of him that afternoon. He would wait for the right moment—before Jack exploded. Phillip smiled as he rode into the breath taking, orange sunrise.

Spupaleena would eventually get her surprise ride to see how the colt would hold up against moving the bawling cows and their spunky calves. She looked forward to the challenge. For now, rest and healing was her main concern. She had plenty of time to get Dusty into shape for the next race. She thought a moment.

Wait, the next race is two weeks away. Somehow, Lord, I have to make that race!

Delbert was fast asleep in his cradle, and Hannah was humming by the fire, rocking her baby doll, who wore the exact same clothing and bandaging as her auntie.

Spupaleena put her fork down and wiped her mouth with the back of her hand.

"Did you get enough to eat?" Elizabeth asked, glancing at her. She raised her eyebrows. "We need to work on that!"

Spupaleena looked at her sheepishly. "Kewa, lim lumt, that was delicious." She sat at the table thumbing through the family Bible. "I wish I could read."

"We can work on it. I know what I taught you before isn't enough, but I could send lessons home with you. We'll figure something out." Elizabeth swiped a strand of sweaty hair off her face. The mornings were all too warm and the cooking fire put out too much heat for her indoor chores.

"With any luck, maybe someday." She closed the Bible and pushed it aside.

Elizabeth stood, leaning against the cool metal cook stove. She noticed her friend was a bit subdued. "Everything okay?"

"Yeah." Spupaleena watched Hannah play, wondering if this could ever be a life for her, a wife with a child. Too many times she felt empty. A part of her was missing and she was uncertain if it had to do with having a family of her own or if the sorrow of her family deaths still haunted her. She was unsure if she would ever recover from them. She longed for a mother. Elizabeth was the closest person in her life to fill that void.

"More tea?" Elizabeth sensed the girl had no intentions of sharing her feelings or thoughts so she let things remain unsaid. In time, Spupaleena would share if she wanted to. Elizabeth had learned early on not to rush her friend, only to have things blow up in her face. God was in charge, not her. She would trust and wait.

"Sure, thanks." Spupaleena blinked back tears. "Some with pain relief, please." She hoped the herbs would drown her physical and emotional throbbing. She grabbed herself tight as a twinge of pain set her ribs on fire. She shoved her pathetic self-pity back deep inside where it belonged.

"Comin' up." Elizabeth strode over to the smoldering fire and heated some fresh water.

"So we were interrupted yesterday," Elizabeth mentioned.

Spupaleena winked at Hannah, who was looking at her with uncertainty. "Hungry men, pressing for sure." Both ladies laughed.

"My mistum and Pekam are the same; when hungry, all else comes to a screeching halt."

Elizabeth finished a few more chores before she sat down to have a heart-to-heart talk. She handed her friend a steaming-hot cup.

"Here ya go." Spupaleena reached for her tea.

"I think I need to still work hard, don't you?"

"Of course, hard and smart. God knows the beginning and the end of your life's journey. It's all in his hands. Don't push your way around; let the Holy Spirit work in your heart. Don't give your competition a reason to harass you—at least don't make it worse—just pray for them and let God do the rest."

"Kewa, but if I train hard, I will win. I have to." Spupaleena took a sip of her tea, wincing as the hot liquid burned her mouth.

Elizabeth thought for a bit as she watched the fire die out. She was treading in shallow water. The last thing she wanted was for Spupaleena to explode and run off.

At the same time, Spupaleena was trying to muster up the will to pray for her enemies.

"What's the main reason you want to win?" Elizabeth held her gaze with soft eyes, asking for the truth.

Spupaleena heaved a sigh. "I'm tired of being criticized."

"By whom? Your father?"

"By everyone. I'm sick of people doubting me—my family, other racers, they all try to mold me into something I'm not. They want me to pick berries and settle down to work." Spupaleena shook her head so hard, the cranial pain and bruised ribs felt like a knife piercing straight through to the bone. She sucked in a breath, and her hand flew up to her forehead.

"Spup," Elizabeth said gently. "Who are you riding for?" She waited patiently for her dear friend to collect herself and answer. Elizabeth sat, fingering the towel in front of her. This question needed to be answered, not for Elizabeth, but for Spupaleena.

"I'm riding for God," she whispered through clenched teeth. She stared at the floor with pursed lips. A moment later, she took a gulp of the cooled tea. Elizabeth waited for the herbs to take effect.

"For God. You seem pretty angry. What's really the issue here?" She held out her hands to the girl. "Tell me." She talked in her soft, non-threatening tone.

Elizabeth had an extraordinary way about her when it came to gently easing information out of an unwilling person. She made a point to never judge; her heart was pure and trusting.

Spupaleena shrugged her shoulders, suddenly feeling like a small child.

Hannah sat, watching the whole scene unfold, her emerald eyes round with a hint of distress.

"Are you mad at Hamis-hamis?" Elizabeth was not about to let Spupaleena off so easy. She needed to deal with her fears and frustration, not keep running off in a fit of rage.

"Loot!" Spupaleena snapped.

"Are you hurt because you never were able to say good-bye?" Elizabeth spoke carefully. The tenseness in the room was thick as honey. She had to find the right balance between gentle extraction and exploding emotions.

Tears pooled in Spupaleena's dark eyes, and she turned her head away from Elizabeth. She sat back and laced her fingers together in her lap.

She breathed in, choking on her words. "I...I so badly wanted to tell her that I forgive her." Her tears broke like a dam and slid down her scarlet cheeks. "By the time I found my mistum, she was gone, and Sneena too, and I never got to say good-bye to either of them.

I never got to hold my Tima." She laid her head in her hands and released years of pent up grief.

Elizabeth rose and made her way to Spupaleena. She slid her arms tenderly around her friend and held her lightly to help ease the pain. "I'm so sorry," she whispered. She let Spupaleena cry for a while, praying silently for peace and forgiveness.

Spupaleena sniffed. "I know bitterness will eat my insides. I try not to."

Elizabeth handed her a handkerchief. "It's all right, healing takes time. Admitting your hurt is an important step. You did that. The hardest part is over. Things are out in the open now, and you don't have to stuff your feelings down in the pit of your stomach any longer." Elizabeth pulled up a chair and sat next to her friend. "Talk to God and keep talking to him; don't ever shut him out. He can't help us when we do. I'll be praying for you, you know that."

Spupaleena nodded, wiping her eyes and nose. Putting her elbows on the table, she cradled her throbbing head. Elizabeth stood to fetch her a cool, wet rag.

"I will help you in any way I possibly can." Elizabeth took the girl's hands into her own.

"I know you will. You're such a good friend, and I love you for it," Spupaleena said through hot tears.

"I love you too." Elizabeth cocked her head, her brows furrowed in concern. "Is there something more?"

Spupaleena paused. "It's hard to forgive myself." She sat trembling, and the tears started all over again. "I'm the one who ran away. I should've stayed." She peered at Hannah, who had fallen asleep on the floor cradling her doll.

"Perhaps, but would anything have been resolved?"

"I don't know."

Elizabeth soothingly rubbed Spupaleena's back and let the silence speak to them. The rest of the morning, they talked and prayed. Elizabeth continued to question Spupaleena's motives. She was worried if the girl was just out to prove a point, she could easily lose focus and come up seriously hurt again. One more head injury, and there could be permanent damage. She would have to pray, wait, and trust.

The next morning, Spupaleena was up early and brushing Dusty. Five days of rest were enough. If it was one thing she was reminded of, it was that God had enough mercy and grace for her at the start of every day, and that was a comfort in itself. Her job was to prepare, God would do the rest.

Jack loped up and reined in his four-year-old, red overo gelding he called Zeri. He was young, but self-assured and strong. He would soon make a great cow horse.

"Can't leave us yet." He smiled.

"Why not? Gotta finish trainin' this big boy." Spupaleena put the brush away and hoisted the pad and saddle on Dusty's back.

"Nah, get on and follow me."

"Why? Where we going?" Jack grinned with a piece of grass hanging out of his mouth.

"Surprise, remember? Hurry, poky, we're burnin' daylight."

Spupaleena shook her head and smiled. Putting her moccasin-covered foot in the stirrup, she climbed on her stud and sat tall. She felt confident, knowing her accident was a fluke.

"Well, let's go then." She motioned her head for Jack to take the lead, and off they went.

Jack took the morning and most of the afternoon instructing Spupaleena how to work Dusty on cattle.

"He's lookin' at 'em." Jack motioned his head in the direction of a red and white heifer.

"He feels loose and confident. I think he's enjoying himself," Spupaleena said, nodding in agreement.

"Go in and cut out a calf and let him get a good look. Don't push him too hard then take him away and bend him some more; can't do enough of that. The softer he is, the safer he'll be."

"Kewa, he's beginning to trust me again."

"He looks good and light. You make a good team, almost dancin'," Jack said, then winked. He was impressed with her swift improvement.

His comment made her cheer inside—to dance—that being her finish line.

A couple more days with Jack and she would head back to her own village. She was anxious to get back in the race.

"You're back, huh?" Skumhist was less than impressed with his daughter's erratic behavior. He had just returned from his trip to the falls—a successful one at that. Heaps of salmon had been harvested, and good times were had by all. He was in hopes of returning to peace and tranquility for once.

"Kewa, why? You didn't think I ran off, did you?" Spupaleena was attempting to tease her father but could see by the look on his face that he was not amused.

Skumhist snorted. He stood, stretching his stiff back. "Should I? Have you ever run off before?" He gave her a long, penetrating look.

"I'm sorry, mistum. I didn't want to wake you." She folded her arms across her chest and looked at the ground. "Besides, I figured you would tell me to stay." Skumhist walked to his daughter, placing his calloused hands on her petite shoulders.

"Supaleena, *In hamink anwee* ("I Love You"). I worry. We have lost too many. I know I can't stop you from racing and fiddling with your horses, but please be careful." Tears pooled in his tired eyes. "I have been told about your accident." He paused, choking down his emotions. "The Creator has shown me that you are no longer a little girl, but at the same time, you need to be cautious. You're a woman, free to choose your own path in life. I respect that now." Skumhist placed a hand on her shoulder. "Please be alert, and next time, wake me; let me know where you're going and for how long. I can't guess anymore; my heart won't take it. I can't ever imagine losing you."

"I will, mistum, I love you too," she said, her face twisting with emotion. "Please forgive me. Kewa, I'll tell you when and where I'm going from now on. I'm all right, really. I took a fall but am better prepared."

She glanced down and fingered her dress. "I…I plan to leave tomorrow," she whispered, hating to throw that at him so soon, but she had little time left to prepare Dusty for the next race. She needed every spare minute.

Skumhist swallowed hard and nodded his head. He would keep his promise and let her go, not so much trusting in his daughter or her horse, but in the Creator and his strength.

"Where to?" Skumhist folded his hands, making the effort to support her.

"Above the San Po-el. I need time in the woods, hills, and crossing the river."

Skumhist nodded. Never would he be able to corral his daughter. He figured it would be better to support Spupaleena than fight with her, pushing her further away.

"I dreamt last night that you…" Skumhist shifted his weight, mopping the sweat off his face with a tattered scrap of buckskin.

"That I…what is it?" Spupaleena waited patiently.

"That if I didn't let you blossom like the wild flowers, you would wither and leave us for good."

"Loot! I could never leave you like that. With God, there's life and laughter, there's trust and hope. Jesus died for us, mistum, so we could live forever. There's no reason for me to run off again. I've changed. I'm not that selfish little girl anymore."

"Kewa, you've shared that with me. I'll sweat and ask the Creator for wisdom."

Spupaleena hugged her father. "Pray for my safety too."

"I will, I always do."

"Good, now what do you need help with? I have all day." Spupaleena canvassed his work area ready to assist.

Skumhist smiled wide and his eyes lit up. "Are you asking to help me?"

"Kewa." Spupaleena felt joy to see her father's face light up. It had been too long. Smiling, she added, "Kewa, I'm able to help you today. I want to." She was avoiding eye contact, knowing her father was thrilled yet struck with amazement. His daughter actually offering to lend a hand? Yes, she was growing up.

Skumhist shook his head. "Loot, today, we talk. Let's pack some food and go sit by the river. You can tell me about your riding and training; we can work another day. Today, we visit." He grinned, knowing now it was his daughter who was dumbfounded.

Spupaleena stared at her father, wide-eyed. She thought she had heard wrong. Skumhist had never in his life asked her to just sit and chat, let alone about the lazy animals who were nothing but mere nuisances. She was certainly thunderstruck.

She threw her arms around her father and kissed his cheek. She was overflowing with bliss and felt like the little girl who once traipsed the woods, trapping with her adored father. The smile on her face would surely last for days on end and into the next race.

Pekam trotted up to his sister, stud colt in tow. "His cinch is snug, and he's ready to win." Pekam's eyes danced with anticipation, and he hopped up and down from one foot to the other, smiling brightly. One would think the boy was the one racing that day.

"Lim lumt," Spupaleena said. She observed him flittering around like a cricket in a glass jar. "Settle down, you're getting Dusty riled up."

"I can't. This is so exciting!" He eyed the other horses and their half-dressed riders. They all sat atop their massive mounts. Horses were prancing and dancing while riders were yelling at one another to get out of their way.

"Well, then, go run around for a while, get rid of your edginess." Pekam peered at his sister, still smiling, still hopping. "Go!"

She needed the time to reflect on the training she did while away in the San Po-el. She could hardly hear herself think with her brother flittering in her face.

He handed the lead to his sister and darted off, whooping and hollering.

Spupaleena shook her head and snickered. "The owls and bats sleep no more." She did last-minute checks and stretched against tight muscles. She strived to be loose and flexible, better able to relax under saddle.

Moments later, Pekam sprung up to Spupaleena, his chest heaving with each breath. Dusty pricked his ears toward the bouncing ball of fire, and he started prancing in circles.

"Pekam, I said settle down, come on, help me out here." Spupaleena flashed him a dissaproving look, wishing she had her calm and seasoned mare instead. "Didn't get very far." She winked after getting a look at his pouty face. It was tough to get after him; he was so wound up and innocent. She wasn't looking to hurt his feelings, just gear him down a notch or two.

"Let's go, they're lining up."

"Let's go then, but first…" Pekam stopped and stared at her blankly. He slouched, sulking like a five-year-old not getting to go and play with the others.

"Come on!" he said in a whiney voice.

"We pray first."

Pekam threw his arms up and his head back, groaning.

"We have time sintahoos." Spupaleena bowed her head, and Pekam mimicked his sister. "Father God, we thank you for this day. Please know that I ride for you with the right heart, not out of anger or bitterness, but to please *you* and you alone. I ask for safety and wisdom. In Jesus's name, amen."

"And a win!" Spupaleena popped her brother with the tail of her rein as he spun, laughing and hopping in circles.

He let loose a cry that shattered the silence, stretching his arms over his head and twirling like a chicken running from a fox. Then a calming presence came over him as if he suddenly ran out of get-up-and-go. He led the young stallion to the starting area. His head held high, and his chest puffed out like he had already won the race. He had poise not pride, confidence not fear. He deemed his sister could win, would win. If Spupaleena lacked assurance, Pekam had plenty extra and was more than willing to send it her way.

Another racer, no one Pekam recognized, whirled up to him and Dusty, shouting a stream of native insults. The boy rode a smaller gray Appaloosa stud colt. He glared from Spupaleena to Pekam and spit at Dusty. Spupaleena grabbed Pekam's arm before he could lunge at the boy and start a fight.

Dusty pawed, letting out a whinny deep inside his throat, more like a guttural growl. He shook his neck and stomped the ground. His eyes looked wild and ready to take on the intruding rival.

"Whoa, boy," Pekam said in a low, soft voice. He pressed his hand on Dusty's neck.

The gray reared up, striking Dusty on the shoulder as he came down. Dusty spun around, kicking fiercely at his opponent with his hind feet. The gray bared his teeth and sunk them into Dusty's neck. Dusty struggled loose, turned, and struck the gray in the teeth, blood spattering in all directions. The sound echoed, astounding the onlookers.

Chapter 8

Phillip and Jack rode up to the valley where the race was to begin. They saw dust rising like a plume of smoke. Horses squealed in the middle of a crowd. They thought they had heard Spupaleena scream, and then as the crowd parted, a look of horror crossed their faces.

Pekam tried his best to stay in the clear, but Dusty bolted into a dead run. Pekam's hand was twisted in the leather lead, dragging the boy as he bounced off every rock and fallen piece of wood.

Finally, the leather strap broke and released Pekam. He rolled, coming to a halt as his head slammed up against a log. He lay on the ground lifeless and bloody. Spupaleena shrieked and ran. She tripped over her own feet, rolled, and scrambled upright. Without missing a beat, she made her way to her brother.

Spupaleena heard a voice screaming and realized it was her own. She gathered her wits about her and gently shook her brother. "Pekam!" He didn't move.

"Pekam! Wake up, you have to be okay, please, God," she begged.

Phillip and Jack galloped off, hoping to catch up to Dusty. They already knew he could run, and run he did. The stallion was in immaculate shape, so the task at hand would be taxing, but the men were up to it. They split and went their separate ways, intending to arc him around and drive him home. Jack loosed his lariat, ready for the right time.

In the meantime, Pekam was hauled off in a make-shift stretcher and taken to his father's home. Skumhist was beside himself. It was one thing for his daughter to be strong-willed, but to pull her eleven-year-old brother into the middle of things was uncalled for.

"Pekam doesn't deserve this." Skumhist paced his six-foot pit dwelling. They were waiting for the tribal healer to arrive. The boy was sprawled out unconscious on a bed of tule-mats, warming by the fire. Even though the air was warm outside, his flesh was cool. "Where is your God now? How could he allow—"

"Loot! This is not God's doing. He is here with us, mistum." Spupaleena turned her back on her father, fighting back tears. She sighed and turned back around. "If this is anyone's fault, it's mine. I should've led the stallion out myself." She sat by her brother. "God kept him alive," she whispered. Looking up at her father, she spoke softly. "He's here, with all of us, now!" She knelt, stroking the side of his face, embracing her guilt. She began singing quietly to him, willing him to heal.

"Here? Where? Under this blanket? In the fire perhaps? Where is he?" Skumhist waved his hands around his home.

Spupaleena stood, looking at her father, and softened her face. "He's sitting right here with my sintahoos, holding him tightly, stricken with sorrow because one of his beloved creations is hurting—that's where," she said, her voice soft and low.

Skumhist stood tall. "Watch yourself, stumpkeelt!" He glared at his daughter with dark eyes, holding in every bit of anger he could as not to strike her.

"Watch? For what? The truth? I can't think for myself, have my own opinions and beliefs?" She swiped a bead of sweat off her forehead and silently prayed for control, grabbing hold of her braids. She had to lighten her grip or pull them straight out of her head. "I believe God is good. He's here and protecting Pekam. The evil one has tried to wound him; God has intervened and saved his life. I hope someday you will see the truth."

Skumhist shook his head in disgust. He was shocked having considered God as any kind of truth or goodness.

"I'll be back later." She could no longer handle the pressure, the blame. Remorse consumed her, and she had to get some fresh air. She jogged down to the river, following the bank until she was out of breath, and then walked even further. Seeing a nice sandy patch, she stopped and flopped down. Her vision blurred through a pool of pent-up tears.

"Why, Father God? Why did it have to be Pekam? It should have been me," she hollered, not caring if any-

Carmen Peone

one in the village heard. Tears streaked down her face. She curled up in the warm sand and fell asleep to the rhythmic slapping of water. The heat of the sun massaged her arms and legs, inviting her to sleep deeply.

Thundering hoof beats threatened to trample Spupaleena. "Loot!" she screamed. The black ghost rider and his dark stallion were gaining on her, closer and closer. She ran, glancing over her shoulder, her eyes filled with terror. Her chest felt like it was going to explode; one more breath, and it would. Her lungs were on fire, and her legs were rubbery, unable to take one more step. Suddenly, she tripped—rolling over and over; they were gaining on her. Looking up, she gasped. Two hooves hovered above her head coming down…

A female voice sliced through her sleep-dazed brain. "Wake up, you're dreaming."

Elizabeth gently shook the girl, kneeling beside her. Spupaleena's eyes fluttered open, and she squinted against the afternoon sun.

"Elizabeth?"

"Yeah, it's me, honey." Elizabeth ran her fingers over Spupaleena's forehead.

Spupaleena shot up and grabbed her friend. She instantly broke down sobbing. Elizabeth held her tightly, stroking her back like she does with little Hannah when she is sad or hurt.

"Pekam, he's hurt. I don't understand why God let this happen. I should've never let him handle Dusty.

He's too strong, too high-strung. It's all my fault," Spupaleena cried.

"I'm sorry. I came as soon as I heard. It's going to be all right."

Spupaleena pulled away from Elizabeth's hold. "But it just happened. How did you find out?"

"One of Phillip's trapping friends, Jeb McLean, got word to me. They live between our home and Lincoln. Someone he knew was at the race and galloped all the way to his place, and Jeb made it to our cabin, I think in record time." Elizabeth chuckled.

Wiping her eyes dry with the back of her hand, Spupaleena nodded.

"How's your brother doing?"

Spupaleena looked away. "He'll make it."

A baby cried nearby. She craned her neck, peering behind Elizabeth.

"You brought Delbert?"

"Yeah, who else is going to feed him?"

Spupaleena smiled. "I guess you have a point. Where's Hannah?"

"Jeb's wife offered to care for her until Phillip gets back. They have a daughter Hannah's age, so you know the fun those two girls will be having. By the way, where is my husband?"

"Um, I don't know," Spupaleena said, feeling a bit embarrassed for having no concern about the men nor her horse. She had figured they would take care of Dusty while she concentrated on her brother.

Elizabeth stood and reached out her hands to help her friend up. She then went and grabbed up her bundle of flailing baby arms and legs, a blanket, and some food she had packed.

"Hungry?"

"Kind of." Spupaleena rubbed the sleep out of her eyes. She looked at the dirt caked on her arms and legs. "I'm a mess. I'll wash up first." She walked to the river and splashed its coolness on her bare limbs and face. The refreshing water woke her up out of a slumber. She wet her hair, running her fingers through the tangled mess. Once it was smooth, she carefully re-braided her black tresses.

Elizabeth spread out one of her hand-sewn quilts, and the ladies sat and visited and ate and prayed, in that order. Spupaleena hardly felt hungry until she smelled the roast beef and cooked cabbage. Then she proceeded to gobble down two helpings of each. Cold or warm, Elizabeth's cooking was always mouthwatering.

The sun was lowering in the brilliant sapphire sky by the time the ladies packed the remaining lunch and Delbert and Elizabeth's other belongings. Spupaleena packed Delbert while Elizabeth led Buttercup, the palomino mare she had dreamed about for several years. Phillip surprised her with the mare one Christmas. She was handpicked out of Jack's stock, of course, and Elizabeth adored her.

Delbert squealed in delight as they passed a chipmunk scurrying up an old larch tree.

"How do you like the pouch Phillip made for him?" Elizabeth asked, trying to make small talk until they faced Skumhist. It would be good to see him again, only if it were under more cheerful circumstances.

"I like it. He's improving with each child." Spupaleena smiled playfully. "It won't take long to get home; my village is just around the bend." Her throat instantly dried up like the desert, and her palms sweat as her thoughts traveled to the image of the anguish on Skumhist's face. She knew facing her father would be difficult, but it had to be done.

"How is your father?" Elizabeth asked. She decided it would be better to discuss him now, hoping Spupaleena would work through some of her hurt and anger before she came face-to-face with him.

"Yeah, watch out. He's sour about the accident. He's angry at me and God."

"I guess he would be. And I'm sure he's plenty scared." Elizabeth grabbed Spupaleena's hand and squeezed it tenderly. "Don't be too hard on him; he needs some time. He's hurting for his son. It's what us parents do."

"Kewa." Spupaleena pressed her lips together and looked ahead. *Lord, give me patience*, she thought.

"Did you come by yourself?" Spupaleena glanced back.

"Yes, I did," Elizabeth answered, suddenly feeling quite brave. "You doubt me?"

Spupaleena laughed. "Loot! Never."

"I recognize that I'm not as *fearless* as you, but please…" The ladies giggled and placed their arms around each other. "But really, Jack gave me precise directions before he left. His markers practically led me here by themselves."

"I'm glad you're here," Spupaleena admitted.

"Me too."

The two walked in silence the short remainder of the way. Elizabeth gazed at the emerald landscape dotted with budding wildflowers and scampering chipmunks. Spupaleena, on the other hand, fought off her tumbling emotions and sickening feelings taking up residence in her gut.

Chapter 9

An ear-to-ear grin crossed over Pekam's face at the sight of his sister walking through the tule-flap door. It had been a couple days since Dusty bounced him over the rock-covered valley floor.

"Wi, lthkickha!"

"Wi, sintahoos, how're you feeling today?"

"Stronger—ready to help you again—soon." He sat by the fire warming up an herbal tea the tribal healer instructed him to drink in order to eliminate the bruising and increase his stamina.

"Good, relax for now. Elizabeth and I are going to the San Po-el, where the bears gather in the creek, to train and pray for a few days."

Pekam's face dropped. He looked like a puppy who had just been scolded.

"I'll be back soon, don't worry. Phillip will come and fetch Elizabeth and Delbert in a week. It will go by fast."

"It's because I got hurt, isn't it?"

"What are you talking about?" Spupaleena sat down on a tule-mat beside him.

"Mistum got to you, didn't he?"

"Pekam, you have to heal—"

"Didn't he?"

Spupaleena paused, tapping her fingers together, searching for the right words. How could she ever tell her brother that someone else would have to help her? She promised her father, at least for now. It broke her heart, but she promised and refused to break the pact. She needed her father's trust more than Pekam needed to lend a hand.

"Pekam, I won't be gone long, and then we'll talk horses and riding." She felt like she was betraying him, failing to tell the truth, but was she? They really would talk, but she knew it was wrong to get his hopes up. However, it was worse to disappoint her father again.

"Kewa," he said, feeling defeated. He slowly rolled onto his side in need of a more comfortable position.

"Besides, you're gettin' scrawny and need to eat and gain some weight," she said, sending him a silly wink.

Pekam smiled and tossed a moccasin at her playfully.

"Go, have fun without me. I'll be here, laying around, fattening up like a cow for slaughter." He chuckled. His eyes danced as he secretly esteemed his sister. He never could stay mad at her for very long.

"See you soon. I love you, sintahoos." Spupaleena held his gaze. Pekam's face blazed red, but inside, his heart warmed. She had never said those words to him.

"You too," he said, his voice low and awkward.

Spupaleena turned and walked out. She chuckled knowing her brother was embarrassed. Yet he needed to hear those three powerful words.

Elizabeth was outside waiting. "Ready?"

"Almost, I have to grab a few more things, and we're off."

Elizabeth turned to see Skumhist approach. He held his hand out to her, and she took it in hers.

"You are good to my stumpkeelt, lim lumt," Skumhist said earnestly. His eyes shone with held-back tears.

Elizabeth tightened her grip. "You're welcome. She's special to me, like a sister." She looked deep into his eyes, understanding, as a mother, his fears and frustration.

Skumhist simply nodded. No words were necessary. They understood one another completely.

"I'll take care of her while we're gone," she added.

"Kewa, I believe you will." He patted Delbert's pudgy little fingers. The toddler looked at the strange man and smiled.

"I'm glad Pekam is gaining strength. He's a strong, good boy."

"Kewa." A hawk screeching overhead caught his attention. He watched the bird for a bit and then looked back at Elizabeth. "But he is foolish with the horses, just like his sister."

Elizabeth shifted her hefty son to the other hip. "She's talented. I hope someday you can realize that—"

"I know," Skumhist interrupted. "I don't deny it." He crossed his arms in front of his chest.

"What is it?" Elizabeth asked encouragingly. "Tell me, please."

He peered at her intently. "I'm…I'm afraid. When my stump keelt ran off, I thought she was dead. I never thought I would see her again."

"I understand."

"Do you?" Skumhist cocked his head to the side.

Elizabeth nodded. "I thought Phillip was dead when he didn't return from Lincoln. Yes, my friend, I do understand." She pulled the baby close. "I have lost a child, a son. He was only a baby…" Her voice trailed off, and she saw the picture of her deceased infant that was imbedded in her memory.

Skumhist's eyes widened. "I didn't know. I'm sorry."

Elizabeth searched his face. "We can't live in fear. Fear is not of God." She rocked Delbert trying to sooth his fidgety self.

"What do you mean?" Skumhist never heard that before. He actually thought the opposite.

"God has given us a spirit of power, love, and self-discipline. When we look to him, we have his strength and don't have to rely on our own."

Skumhist nodded in agreement. "Maybe you're right. We shouldn't live in fear, but it's hard to let her grow up."

"Of course it is. You love her and only want to protect her. You're a good father, Skumhist." His face lit up at the sound of those words: *you're a good father*. He was beginning to doubt himself.

"You're a good friend. You teach her well."

"Not me, Skumhist, but God. I simply support her."

He said nothing.

"I'll pray for you and Pekam," Elizabeth said genuinely.

"Lim lumt, you're a strong woman of faith. Be safe."

"Thank you, we'll speak soon." He nodded to her, ending the conversation.

Skumhist smiled, turned, and walked away. It was time to check on his son.

The horizon was filled with jade colored larch, fir, and pine trees. The grass was tall and lush. The swollen San Po-el River rushed wildly, meandering down the valley. It's bubbling snake-like appearance sparkled in the summer sunshine.

The ladies reined in their horses, soaking in the breathtaking view. The jagged, basalt cliffs invited years of storytelling. Elizabeth breathed deeply, letting her lungs expand in the fresh, floral air. She shaded her eyes against the sun.

"This is spectacular," Elizabeth said, glancing around in awe.

"Kewa, you should see it come fall when the leaves turn. Vibrant colors of red, orange, yellow, and gold are splashed everywhere you look."

Elizabeth had a hard time tearing her eyes from the rugged beauty. She could imagine the radiant hues as if a painter took his brush and flung pigment on the foliage, allowing originality of each individual leaf.

"Camp is upstream, not far from here." Spupaleena stroked Dusty's neck, keeping their distance from the mare. For being just three, he was a gentleman around Buttercup. "Let's get going, we'll make it before dusk."

Once the trio reached the campsite, they unloaded their supplies and set up. They had to make the most of their time before dark.

As the girls set up the tent, Elizabeth came up with a daily schedule. Things would have to run smoothly in order for Spupaleena to get the most of her training time without taxing herself or the stallion. Together, they came up with a plan: Elizabeth would do all the cooking and chores while Spupaleena concentrated on training and caring for Dusty. With an eight-month-old baby, she would have her hands full camped by running water but would manage.

Spupaleena decided to get in a quick ride before the sun set. She saddled Dusty and led him over to Elizabeth, who was relaxing by a roaring fire. The air had brought in a chill; besides, a crackling fire was always pleasing.

"Oh, watch out for two things," Spupaleena announced, stifling a grin.

"Huh? What danger looms ahead?" Elizabeth replied playfully as she made last-minute adjustments to Delbert's makeshift cradle.

Spupaleena chuckled. "Bears and rattlers."

Elizabeth jumped to her feet, nearly tumbling into the blazing fire. Spupaleena laughed. Elizabeth glared at her, not real impressed with her practical joke.

"Not too funny."

"I'm not kidding," Spupaleena said, growing serious. "Hope you brought your pistol. Oh, and keep Buttercup and Delbert close," she said over her shoulder, walking away with the stallion close behind.

Elizabeth frantically scoped the area. Her eyes darted from rock, to stump, to fallen log.

"Great, bears and snakes. I can handle the bears, but snakes? She probably knew I wouldn't come, having been told there are rattlers around. Darn her." Elizabeth hurriedly checked on Delbert then continued searching the area wide-eyed, reaching for a stick, trusting it to protect her. A shiver ran down the length of her spine. "I hate snakes." She snatched up the baby and headed for the Colt .45 Phillip had tossed into her pack.

Elizabeth combed through her satchel until she felt the cold steel rub against her hand. She was thankful her husband had insisted on her taking the weapon. She would sleep better knowing a loaded pistol was ready for any type of intruder, weather it slithered or growled.

Daylight came early. Spupaleena woke up to the smell of rosehip tea and pancakes. She stretched her stiff muscles and stood. Peering out the tent flap, she caught a glimpse of the soft salmon-colored sky.

"Where did you get that?" Spupaleena asked, sniffing that sweet, familiar aroma wafting in the air.

"Your father made sure I brought along your favorite tea." Elizabeth looked up and smiled.

A quiver tickled the back of her neck at the thought of her father's loving gesture. Once her tummy was satisfied, Spupaleena saddled Dusty and headed out for her morning session. She would ride him under saddle for the first day or so and then switch to bareback.

She preferred bareback and the closeness and trust it gave the two of them. For now, she focused on getting Dusty in shape. Together, they traversed the terrain, climbing mountains, swimming ponds and the bubbling San Po-el River, jumping fallen logs and working on creating a solid stop. Most racers ignored teaching their horses to stop, but Spupaleena strived for total control of the twelve-hundred-pound animal. She was not interested in having part of him; she wanted all of him, or nothing.

It was nearing dusk when Spupaleena decided to trot one more lap on the trail she had traveled that morning. It would be a nice cooldown for the colt. There was a nice, grassy piece that would be kind to his legs and a small stream to pause for a cool drink. Riding him twice a day was strengthening him physically, but at the same time wearing him down.

On impulse, she decided to toss off the saddle and ride bareback. Jack had mentioned that the colt had yet to be ridden without a saddle, but Spupaleena felt he was far enough along there would be no problems. He displayed great confidence, and so did she. Taking a running two-step-hop, she effortlessly pulled herself up on Dusty's back.

He stood calm, so she took the time to lie on his back and rub him all over. She felt him relax and it showed as he hung his head low. After a bit, she sat upright and grabbed hold of his mane and urged him into a walk. She circled him a couple times and then nudged him into a trot. Spupaleena smiled; she thought his stride was smooth under saddle, but in reality, he floated bareback. It was as if they were barely moving.

Feeling a bit spry, she asked for a little more. They were now loping, and it was as if they had ridden this way all along. They turned a corner on the rocky trail and Dusty slowly took a greater hold of the bit and sped up. Spupaleena was concerned but let him go; he was born to run. The warm wind whipped in her face and she felt free.

In the heat of excitement, the colt started kicking up his hind legs, and before she knew it, was in a crow-hopping buck. Spupaleena held on tightly with her legs and tried to gain control with her rein, but did so to no avail. The colt twisted to the left, and she flew off to the right, hitting the ground with a thud. Thankfully, she landed on her shoulder in a patch of grass. However, Dusty kept going.

Again, the colt had no intentions of slowing down. Like Spupaleena had admitted time and time again, he loved to run. She stood and brushed the dirt and grass off of her leggings and dress. She was glad to wear plain doeskin without fancy beadwork or shells that could easily be torn off.

Assuming the colt had more than likely galloped back to camp, she headed to retrieve the saddle. She was grateful it was light and compact, not like Jack's bulky roping saddle. The good news: yes, Dusty probably headed down the mountain to Buttercup; the bad news: Elizabeth would see the rider-less horse and fret.

She had a ways to walk out, and only by the grace of God would her horse be just around the corner.

Spupaleena took the time walking home to commune with her Creator. She had just gulped a good dose of humility straight from God's glass. She not only asked him for forgiveness but asked him to reveal any other selfishness and recklessness or even pride she failed to see. It was necessary to shed it all in order to ride for her Lord and Savior. Otherwise, he would keep allowing her to get dumped in order to grab her attention. "I'm all yours," she said, lifting her hands and face to the heavens.

It was black as coal with the clouds shading the light from the stars and moon when Spupaleena finally entered camp. The air was cool, but not as icy as Elizabeth's expression in the light of the glowing fire. Even from a distance she could see the worry and anger all mixed into one frigid look. Elizabeth was pacing around the fire, stick in hand. From a distance, it looked as though that was the weapon of choice for Spupaleena the moment she was spotted.

"Oh, Lord, Creator God, help me. Help Elizabeth understand the situation and let her put that stick down, In Jesus's name, amen."

The leaves crackled under her buckskin feet. Elizabeth turned her head, dropped the stick, and ran for Spupaleena. She put her arms around the girl and held her tight.

"I was so worried. Are you all right? What happened? Dusty showed up, and you were nowhere to be seen—"

"I'm not hurt, really," Spupaleena interrupted. "Sit down, and I'll tell you about it. He just got away from me. It's okay, I promise."

Spupaleena could see the relief written all over her friend's face. Poor thing, how many times did her friends have to pick her off the ground and dress her wounds? At least this time there was not even one scratch, which really amazed her, considering her past.

Elizabeth poured Spupaleena a steaming cup of rosehip tea. The pair then sat by the fire as Spupaleena retold the scene.

"I'm so glad you're not hurt. From now on, we… you, when you're alone, will pray for protection…and wisdom….and patience…"

"Kewa, I…we will." Spupaleena looked at her friend in admiration and genuine love. She was fortunate to have a friend who took such good care of her. "I promise to never take him for granted again. I need to quit allowing him to take control of the rein. He's so powerful. I have to grab his attention before he even thinks about it. It was my fault."

Elizabeth waved the stick around as she spoke. "Did you really learn anything from this?" She pointed the stick at the girl's chest. "And…and you have to show me…or draw me a map in the dirt of where you'll be riding. I can't believe we didn't do that earlier. I'm so upset, you could've been seriously hurt again…another head injury…don't you know that could mess you up?" She took a breath, nodding, waiting for Spupaleena to agree. She pointed the stick at her, looked at it, and threw it down in the dirt.

Spupaleena nodded. "Of course."

"Good…okay then." Elizabeth eased herself to the ground and leaned back against the log.

It was hard for Spupaleena to admit her shortcomings out loud but knew it was the right decision. "Kewa, I already confessed my selfishness to God and asked him to reveal any other attitude that separates us." She moved the stick further away with her foot.

"And he will, trust me." The girls laughed and then visited by the fire for a little longer before calling it a night. They would return home in a couple more days, just in time for the next race.

Chapter 10

"<u>Lth</u>kickha, I don't see Hahoola<u>who</u>. He must have chickened out knowing you have a new and powerful horse. He's probably hiding in his bed, curled up like a **<u>k</u>oo<u>k</u>yuma o<u>h</u>u<u>h</u> teelut** ("Tiny baby")." Pekam laughed too loudly at his own joke. He was as energetic as a hungry hummingbird, flitting around from flower to flower, talking in circles. He made Spupaleena dizzy as she attempted to finish grooming the stallion. Dusty shook his head, pawing at the ground and kicking up dust. Spupaleena stroked his neck and flashed her brother a sharp look. He sat on a nearby log, trying his best to hold still, yet wiggling his legs.

"Apparently, Quiy S<u>k</u>et came up lame, so he's not entered," Spupaleena said coolly. Pekam hopped back up. Part of her was disappointed, but the other part could care less. It was easier to maintain some sort of humility with his absence. She could keep her mouth shut and her attitude in check. It would be good practice until they met again.

Pekam suddenly stopped dead in his tracks. "How come you all the sudden don't care? He's the enemy. The one to squash like a worthless bug."

"God got my attention while I was away. If I don't honor him, there is no glory."

"What are you talking about?"

"I'm saying that after I gave my heart to Jesus, I need to start showing it. I've been self-centered and a bad example to you. I got you hurt—"

Pekam snapped his fingers at her. "You didn't get me hurt, it was my fault. I should've—"

"*I* should have. I'm not going to argue. The point is I need to live in a way that God would be pleased with me, or what's the point?"

"I-I prayed a lot when I was hurt." Pekam's face grew solemn. He crouched down and picked up a handful of pebbles, tossing them into the brush, one by one.

"Time to line the horses up, Spupaleena, hurry," a cousin announced.

"Coming…" She turned to her brother. "We'll talk more tonight when I can listen to you. I want to hear what you have to say, okay?"

The boy nodded. "Lim lumt." He stood to hold the rein.

Pekam held Dusty as Spupaleena climbed up. The young stallion could feel the crowd's energy. He began to paw and dance in anticipation. His ears honed into the nearby stallions, also prancing while they lined up. Spupaleena tugged on the rein, but Pekam held on tight.

"Aren't you going to pray?" Pekam bowed his head.

Spupaleena smiled, shocked he remembered. "Oh, thanks. Please, Lord, let us have a good and safe ride. I ask for protection, not to win, but just run like you would have us. Thank you for your forgiveness and love, in Jesus's name, amen."

"Amen, see you at the finish line." Pekam let go of the rein and loped off into the eager crowd. He sprinted to the finish rope, wanting a clear view of victory. He squeezed his way to the front, not caring if he offended anyone. He wanted to see his sister cross, way ahead of the others, he was sure.

As Spupaleena made her way to the starting rope, she was amazed at how calm Dusty was compared to the other horses. She wondered if this was a good or bad sign. She had trained him, reconciled with God, and prayed beforehand; now all she could do is trust, and hang on.

She heard the faint cry and kicked Dusty into an immediate gallop. He wasted no time. It was as if he had been doing this since he was a yearling. He pulled ahead and settled into a smooth and steady gait. Spupaleena relaxed into his rhythm and let him stretch out and run.

After a bit, she glanced behind her and was startled to see no one near them. She realized Dusty was fast, but was he really this far ahead? She peered over her shoulder a second time and saw that it was true. She felt the power as he galloped on the soft green earth.

His breath was a steady swooshing sound. They moved together in a smooth rocking motion, rapidly eating up the ground. It was not long before they hit the finish rope and slowed to a stop. Just as she was about to turn and trot back to the starting point, the other horses bolted past, hardly able to slow down.

Spupaleena smiled. She was glad to have put the effort into training Dusty to stop and stand still. She glanced up, and the other competitors were still going strong. Thick dust swirled around her. She had to cover her mouth and nose, squeezing her eyes shut until it all settled enough that she could suck in air without choking. "Watch my attitude, keep me lowly, please, God," she mumbled. The grin was still on her blackened face, but for gratifying the Creator, not herself. "Thank you, Father God. I race for you and you alone."

Pekam came dancing and twirling up to her. He whooped so loud her ears rang. He looked and sounded like a hen on fire. "You won! I knew you would," Pekam said as he stroked Dusty's neck.

"We did win, and it feels good. He worked hard and earned it." Spupaleena ran her fingers through his black, thick mane. Dusty stood with his head lowered, his soft eyes half-mast. He was still breathing rapidly but knew he had done well.

"You ran a good race," Skumhist said as he walked up to the trio. Spupaleena swung around. She could hardly believe her eyes.

"Mistum?" Spupaleena slid off her horse and handed the rein to her brother.

Skumhist gathered his daughter into his arms. His eyes wet with pride. She let his embrace warm her heart. *Thank you, God*, she prayed silently.

"I didn't realize you were such a strong rider. I'm impressed," Skumhist said.

"Did you watch the whole race?" Pekam asked, actually standing still.

"Kewa, I did, from over there." He motioned to the top of a nearby hill. "I wanted the best view to see my daughter's triumph."

Spupaleena stared at her father. She questioned why he had a sudden change of heart. She felt a hint of mistrust, hoping her father's reaction was not one of the enemy's tricks. "I'm glad you came."

"I know as your mistum that you need support, not condemnation. You're a woman now, and I'm ready to encourage you, not tear you down."

Spupaleena was starved for his verification, but now that she had it, she was uncertain how to handle it. She was used to defending herself and arguing with him. She prayed for understanding and her own heart transformation.

"I realize Pekam's accident was not your fault. It could have happened to anyone." He held his daughter's hands in both of his. "Elizabeth helped me see things the way they are supposed to be. She's a good friend."

Spupaleena merely nodded. She fought back fresh tears. Glancing sideways, she caught her brother's huge, gleaming smile on his dirt, streaked face. She wanted to celebrate not cry, even if the tears were healing. This was a big win for her; she was victorious on the grassy stretch, but more importantly in her father's love. This was a good day.

"Big success today, huh?" Phillip asked. The Gardener family made it just in time to see her cross the finish rope. They spotted Skumhist on the rocky hill, and he motioned them to come and watch. After tethering their horses, they climbed up and settled the children down with a treat. They literally looked up and saw the pair thundering down the lane and cross the line.

Hannah jumped up and down in delight, clapping her hands. She hollered nearly loud enough for her auntie to hear. The girl scrambled out of her mother's embrace and dashed off to find her hero, but Skumhist was quick enough to pluck her off the ground and clutch her safely in his arms. She squirmed and screeched as he attempted to soothe her with his native tongue.

They all met Spupaleena back at the staging area. Everyone hugged and shook hands, then helped her collect the winnings and pack them on horses for the return home. She was going to have to sell or give away much of the loot. It was piling high on the dirt floor, lining the inside rim of her home.

The Gardners traveled to the race to see Spupaleena compete but also spend time with her family. Her heart raced with excitement. The two families were all together for the first time. She prepared the perfect meals, not letting Elizabeth help in any way. Elizabeth was told to rest, it was her vacation. It was Spupaleena's turn to host, and she was going all out—fresh salmon, camas, wild potatoes, and carrots.

For the next couple of days, the families let the horses rest. They fished, swam, and played. Even Skumhist enjoyed the time off. One evening, they sat outdoors visiting, enjoying the warm, crackling fire. The orange glow soothed their tired bodies as did the nightly songs of the crickets resonating in the distance.

"Phillip, how would you like to come and check a couple traps with me and Pekam in the morning?" Skumhist asked. He looked forward to the company since he mostly walked the line alone these last few years. "I have a few closer one's south of the village."

"I would love to." Phillip broke out into a wide grin. It had been far too long since he was able to tramp around chasing wild game. Spupaleena had told him many stories of traipsing out in the woods with her father, and soon, he would be able to experience some of them. His heart beat sped up just thinking about it.

They talked for a while longer, and then everyone retired for the night. Phillip was so thrilled he barely slept. He felt alive and looked forward to the adventure and his time with Skumhist. He was sure to learn some new and simpler techniques. Hopefully he could even set something up close to his cabin once he returned home, even teaching Delbert the ways of a trapper.

The sun peeked over the mountains when the guys opened their sleepy eyes. They ate a quick breakfast of potato cakes and berries and then quietly departed. They walked quickly and quietly through the forest and were soon approaching the first snare. Phillip tried to guess what might be captured inside.

"I'm glad you're coming with us," Pekam said to Phillip.

"Me too. I hope we see a lot of wildlife." Phillip patted the boy on the back.

"My stump̲keelt has told me you trapped before your accident." Skumhist said as he studied the forest floor for fresh animal tracks.

"Yes, I did, but it became too difficult to get around with my bum leg. I moved too slowly. But God has blessed me with a good friend and partner, and I'm now a cattleman." Phillip chuckled.

Skumhist nodded. "I'm glad you're able to work and provide for your family."

"Thank you, I am too. My wife has been good to me and supportive with the cows and horses. I don't know what I'd do without her."

"Yes, she's a good woman and good to Spupaleena, especially since her mother and grandmother are no longer with us. I'm thankful for your wife." The deaths were still tender to his heart. They walked to the next snare in silence.

Skumhist turned his thoughts to trapping with Spupaleena when she was a little girl. She always did have a way with animals. He admired her love and respect for them. He wished he could tell her so but failed to muster up the courage. He was unsuccessful at understanding why. It just was not his character to talk so intimately with others.

"So you told my l̲thkickha about this Jesus?" Pekam asked. Skumhist flashed him a look that would knock any rider off his horse. "What?" he whined, shrugging his shoulders, a smirk crossed his face.

Phillip laughed, oblivious to the death-threatening look Skumhist gave his son. "No, it was actually my wife. They had many conversations while she stayed with us. When your sister first came to stay with us, she suffered through nightmares, but we prayed over her, and it seemed to help."

Skumhist stopped dead in his tracks, turning to Phillip. "Help? How?" he asked.

Phillip faced the man. "Well, I'll tell you, there's power in the name of Jesus alone, and when someone prays according to his will, not our own, he *moves*. Especially when two or more come together, it's healing and many times comforting. Her nightmares quit haunting her, and she began to ask about the God we worship."

"I asked Jesus into my heart, but I haven't told Spupaleena yet. She's going to be happy, I know it," Pekam said, jumping off a log. Good thing they weren't hunting, the animals would be long gone with all the noise the boy made.

"Good for you, Pekam. Yes, your sister will be very happy."

Skumhist picked up a stick, thinking about their conversation. He just wasn't sure he believed as they did. Why would such a powerful God need to die for another? It sounded like a weak God to him.

"What about you, Skumhist, have you thought much about God?"

"At first, I fought it. We have our own ways and beliefs, but watching the change in Spupaleena and the love your wife shares with others, I'm considering knowing this Jesus of yours." Skumhist stopped. "Will you tell me more? I just don't know."

Phillip placed a gentle hand on his new friend's arm and smiled. "Of course I will."

They walked and talked, stopping here and there as Phillip shed light on God's truths.

It was a good day. They even came home with a martin and a rabbit for supper.

As the trio approached the village, a relative came running up to them.

"Your wife is not doing good…the baby…there's something wrong," he said in his native tongue, panting and motioning to Spupaleena's home.

Phillip and Skumhist looked at each other. Skumhist translated the conversation in English but no translation was needed, Phillip understood the man's meaning; he knew something was terribly wrong. Phillip felt as though someone had just punched him in the gut. He wanted to run, but his body remained stiff. Skumhist was able to catch his attention, and they sprinted to where Elizabeth was resting, Pekam close behind.

Simillkameen met them at the door. "Loot, you stay out here." She held up her hand in front of the men. Skumhist again translated.

Phillip's expression pleaded with her. "I want to see my wife." Phillip's face was as white as snow. The woman shook her head.

Skumhist held his shoulder. "We can wait out here."

Phillip shook his head. "I need to see her."

"Let the woman work. She knows the ways of the women." Skumhist motioned to the healer. "Elizabeth will be taken good care of."

Hearing their voices, Spupaleena emerged through the flap door. "Elizabeth is having pains. It's not time for the baby to come yet." There was more, but seeing the panic on Phillip's face, she decided not to reveal too much just yet. "She still has three months left. Simillkameen will give her some herbs to stop the pain and keep the baby inside." She peered at Phillip, looking him square in the eyes. "She'll be okay. When Simillkameen is finished, you can go in and see her. It won't be long."

Phillip sat down on a nearby log and put his head in his hands, saying a prayer for his wife. When he was done he looked back up at Spupaleena. "Thank you," he whispered, his voice thick with emotion. He watched her for a moment then asked, "What else is wrong?" His face pleaded for the truth.

Spupaleena's eyes widened. She knew it was stupid to try and hide anything from Phillip.

She nodded and grabbed her braids. "Her body is swelling and…" Her gaze dropped to the ground.

Carmen Peone

"And what?" he insisted.

Spupaleena looked at the ground through wet eyes. "She…she was convulsing…"

Phillip could do nothing but weep. He had already lost one baby. How could he lose two and perhaps the love of his life?

"Simillkameen knows what to do. She'll be just fine, and now she needs rest and quiet." Spupaleena could hardly stand to see Phillip this upset. His pain was written all over his face, and his eyes reflected a sadness she had never seen before, not even when Elizabeth thought Phillip was dead.

"Come, let's pray," Skumhist offered, taking a seat beside him. He placed his hand on his back and began to ask the Creator for healing for Elizabeth and comfort for his friend. Having already lost a wife and child, he was able to empathize with Phillip.

When the prayers were done, Skumhist stood, helping his friend to his feet. Spupaleena flashed her father a look of surprise. Skumhist nodded at his daughter, turned, and escorted Phillip to his home.

"What's going on?" Spupaleena asked, turning to face Pekam.

"Mistum is thinking good thoughts about our God."

Spupaleena raised her eyebrows. "Our?"

"Yes, our. I wanted to tell you before the race, but we were cut off, and you had to go and line up."

Spupaleena squealed and gave her brother a huge bear hug.

"I'm so happy for you!"

"Yeah, I told them you would be." Pekam beamed as his sister wrestled around with him playfully.

Spupaleena grew somber. "I need to check on Elizabeth. Take care of your catch for mistum, will you?"

"Kewa, I'll pray for Elizabeth too. Will she be okay?"

"God will take care of her," Spupaleena said, hiding her concern.

Chapter 11

"I don't know how I'm going to keep Dusty in shape and ready for the upcoming races." Spupaleena shook her head. Her expression filled with distress.

"Don't worry. Jack, Pekam, and myself, we'll all help," Phillip said, looking at Jack and nodding for support. "I know you want to help take care of Elizabeth, and that's okay. She wants to stay here with you and Simillkameen, which will be good. She needs help with the children. I appreciate your willingness to do it."

"I know you do. It's the least I can do. She was there for me and…" Spupaleena turned away from Phillip, wiping away a tear that slipped out of her red, tired eye.

"Everything will be okay. You don't always have to act so tough. You're a girl, remember? You cry. It's what girls do," Jack said, trying to lighten the tone.

Spupaleena laughed. "Kewa, I'm getting that. Don't like it, but getting it."

"You have a tender heart, my friend; you have compassion, which is a gift from God. Others are hardhearted and don't display much sympathy. I'd rather have someone like you around because it's evident you care. It's comforting." Phillip hobbled over to a stump and sat down. He winced at the shooting pain traveling up his nub leg. He was plain worn out.

She shrugged her shoulders. "I guess...lim lumt anyway." She glanced up at Phillip. "I'll get you something for the pain." He smiled and nodded. A little relief would be welcoming.

Pekam had been outside the tule-mat door, which unsuccessfully held their voices at bay. He felt a deep sense of urgency to aid his sister. She was always there for others, and now it was his turn to lend a hand. He would be the one to train Dusty. Pekam had all the confidence he needed to handle the willful stallion, or so he thought; yes, he could get the job done. Jack and Phillip had more important tasks at hand, and this was a way he could show his love and devotion for his sister.

His mind was made up.

It was late that night. His buckskin pack was loaded with food and clothing. He lay in bed, restless as ever, and waited. He waited for his father to fall asleep. He waited for the village to settle into the night. He waited until he could slip away undetected.

Silence came quickly. Only the sound of distant coyotes, yapping for their next victim, echoed through the cloudless night. The moon was high, and a canopy of twinkling stars covered the warm summer evening. A nearly full moon would make traveling easy and quick.

Pekam sat up, allowing his eyes to adjust. He saw the outline of his father, who was sound asleep on his tulemats, covered with a light blanket he had traded for with the white people at the falls. He looked peaceful. The boy rose out of his bed, snatched his bag, and tiptoed out into the night. He figured as tired as his father was, sleep would be deep; sneaking would be simple. A smile crossed the boy's face. He peered around, double-checking for any movement. He saw none and headed for the corral. Pekam felt electrified as the adrenaline rushed through his body.

He could see the glow of the horses' eyes as he neared the corral. They shuffled softly, studying the boy as he came closer. Never had a human come to them in the middle of the night. They nosed him, searching for a treat. He had none, only a halter. He placed it on Dusty's head and led him out. Rainbow whinnied in protest as she was left behind.

"Shh, don't wake anyone up. We won't be gone but a few days." Pekam stroked her neck and nose. He looked around for something to quiet her and settled on a handful of grass, pleading for silence.

Standing by the horse's side, he effortlessly hopped on the colt's back and picked his way out of the village and into the forest. Dusty put his nose down, examining the ground and carefully placing each foot where it should go, dodging big rocks and downed wood. Pekam prayed his father would show him some amount of lenience, asking God to fill his family's hearts with understanding. Shivering from the cool, early morning air, and no doubt his excitement, the boy leaned closer to the horse's neck for added warmth. He took hold of the rein and picked up to a trot, planning his next step.

Spupaleena awoke to her angry father's voice. He was hollering, but she hardly made sense of the words. The tone in his voice alluded to irritation mixed with frustration. Tossing her blanket aside, Spupaleena strode outside. Phillip, who was attempting to calm him down, was talking to her father. She rushed over to them and caught the end of a horrifying impression.

She looked at the corral and saw that Dusty was gone. She looked at her father with round eyes and saw the rage in his own.

"Oh, no," Spupaleena said.

"I can't believe he has done this." Skumhist ran his fingers through his thick, course hair. He started graying the year Spupaleena left, and she swore she could see more emerge right in front of her.

"Why did he take him?" Spupaleena felt as if she would vomit.

"I have no idea. He must've known you were worried about the upcoming race and keeping Dusty fit." Skumhist held his temper in check, even though he felt like he could just pack up and leave, letting the kids fend for themselves. He was fed up and full of rage—not a promising combination. Everyone stood, looking at one another, contemplating the next move.

The silence was awkward.

"I hope he didn't overhear us talking yesterday," Phillip added.

Spupaleena caught his gaze and gasped. "I bet he did."

"I'll go after him—"

"Loot, he wants to be a man, we'll let him. He'll learn fast that being a boy is much more amusing." Skumhist started to walk off and turned, pointing a finger at his daughter. "Let's see if your God does protect him and hopefully teaches him a valuable lesson."

Spupaleena and Phillip looked at one another and back at Skumhist as he marched toward the river in search of a secluded place to pray. They stood in silence for a few minutes, watching him walk away. Spupaleena was unsure if she should obey her father and stay, or take Rainbow and set out in search of her brother.

"You need to stay. Your father said to let him grow up, honor his word," Phillip said. He leaned against the gate blocking her way. Spupaleena kicked the dirt.

"What if he gets hurt?" She lifted her exasperated gaze to Phillip.

"We'll let God take care of that."

Spupaleena shook her head. "I don't know…"

Phillip pointed his finger to the village. "Go."

Spupaleena sighed. "I didn't say I was going anywhere."

"I've known you long enough." He smiled. "Come on. Let's check on Elizabeth and the kids. Hannah's been asking for you."

She nodded. "Let me tether Rainbow, and I'll be right behind you."

"How about I tether her, and you go see how my family's getting along." He smiled down at her, and she got the hint. She did as Phillip asked, but pouted nonetheless, as she stomped off.

"I see what you're doing here," she said over her shoulder, irritated as ever. She glared back at him and flicked her hand at the ground. "I'm going."

Spupaleena felt an urgency to pray for her brother as she walked to her pit house. She prayed for his safety and asked God to let her know if she needed to go after him. She asked the Holy Spirit to make it crystal clear, and she would be on her way. All she heard was silence.

Pekam woke up feeling fresh and ready to exercise the colt. The previous day, he spent most of this time traveling to a place he was satisfied with, a place his sister would have picked. After taking many wrong turns, he finally found the perfect training grounds, one with plenty of hills, deadfall, and water. He contemplated riding bareback, but thought better of it. He was unfamiliar with Dusty, and he refused to do anything that would harm Spupaleena's chances of winning. He had to do what his sister did and how she did it, imitating her every move. They rode in a similar fashion, so he thought the task at hand should be easy.

After a quick breakfast of dried moose meat and berries, Pekam saddled up Dusty. They were south of camp; he looked around and thought for sure they were at the gate of hell. The country was rugged and desertlike, and no one was remotely close, but there were plenty of obstacles to maneuver around. His only motive was to keep the colt in shape and sharp-minded.

As they trotted about, Pekam became more and more comfortable. He could see why his sister raved about the horse. He was smooth, light, and powerful. He had yet to let the horse run full speed; however, the thought rolled around in his head. He convinced himself to keep a steady pace so no one would get hurt, at least that day. Spupaleena would be infuriated if anything happened to Dusty, especially because he would eventually be one of the main breeding stallions.

Glancing up at the sky, Pekam noticed dusk would be coming soon, and black clouds were rolling closer. *Where had the day gone?* he thought. The colt felt jittery so Pekam decided to head back to camp. He walked back, allowing the colt to cool down. He was nearly there when lightning streaked across the sky, and the air cracked around him.

Dusty reared up, but Pekam was able to hang on. He had seen his sister pull him around tight, and that is exactly what he did. They ended up circling all the way back to where he tied up his pack. Pekam questioned whether Dusty would take off in the middle of the night scared, or if he would be there in the morning. Time would tell. He was able to secure the colt before the rain poured down. He ran for cover, praying Dusty would stay put.

One item Pekam forgot was a shelter of some sort. It had been warm outside, and he never dreamed a storm would suddenly show its ugly face. He hunkered down under a tree, but the rain and wind assaulted him anyhow. Pekam looked around, desperately searching for somewhere—anywhere—to get out of the storm.

A blaze of lightning lit up the sky. A sideways glance revealed an overhang under the base of a cliff. He could barely make it out through the debris being slammed around by the whipping gusts of wind. The boy was astonished at his dumb luck, or was it? He rushed over to Dusty and grabbed the colt's lead, hurrying over to the comfort of the ledge. It would have to do. It was enough to cover Pekam completely and most of Dusty. Only a slice of his rump and tail hung out in the squall of the night.

Pekam sat up against the rock wall, shivering. He was feeling a bit meek at this point, not as brave as he once believed himself to be. "God, I'm sorry. Get me through the night, and I'll head back home. I know I shouldn't have taken Dusty, but I just wanted to help my lthkickha. She always helps people. I wanted to do the same for her."

Pekam settled under his blanket, gripped his fingers around the horses lead, and fell asleep—hungry, cold, and miserable.

The morning was bright, and the air smelled like fresh sage. The sky was a deep blue without a single cloud hovering above. Pekam blinked open his sleepy eyes. He saw Dusty just outside of the overhang munching on the clean, wet grass. It made the boy aware of his own grumbling tummy. He stood and walked over to where he abandoned his pack and took out some food. He ate slowly and mournfully, knowing the promise he made to God. He would honor that pact and head home as soon as he took in some nourishment.

Pekam was somewhat relieved knowing he was going home to the safety of his father's protection. Being out on his own was not exactly what he had expected, but he would never admit to being home-sick.

He dreaded meeting his sister and father, knowing he would feel the wrath of them. The closer they got, the sicker he felt. At one point, Dusty craned his neck, looking back at him as if to understand his troubles. Pekam never once thought through the consequences. He was convinced his dedication to Spupaleena would be enough to justify his escapade. Now he was unsure it would carry him anywhere.

As they came into view of the village, he caught sight of his father walking in the woods. He stopped and watched Skumhist talking to someone. Searching for another person, Pekam found no one. Then it dawned on him that perhaps he was talking to God. Pekam swallowed hard, nearly bursting out in tears. At least he wanted to. His first instinct was to turn and kick the horse into a gallop back to the gate of hell. But he froze instead. His father's expression was not what was expected.

"Pekam!" Skumhist hollered, waving his arms.

Pekam sat on the young stallion, dumbfounded. He stared at his father with a gaping mouth. Had his father gone mad? He slid off the animal and walked cautiously toward his father. Skumhist, on the other hand, was happily trotting to his son with a huge smile on his face. Pekam scratched his head.

Skumhist embraced his son. "I'm so glad you're home." Pekam wrapped his scrawny arms around his father. He suddenly understood what God's grace felt like. He saw the change in his father from a heart of anguish to a heart of forgiveness. He figured there would still be some type of consequences, and he would take them like a man.

Spupaleena, on the other hand, marched up; fury plastered her face, which made Pekam turn a red brighter than his sisters. "What have you done? Where is my stallion? I can't believe you had the nerve to take off like that!"

In the distance, children could be heard giggling. Pekam could feel all their little eyes on his back. He knew they were hiding in the bushes listening. He guessed what everyone thought of him.

Spupaleena cleared her throat. Rage twisted in the air, and her face displayed its presence. Pekam forced his attention back to his sister.

You taught me well, he thought but dared not say. Now he knew why his father acted so loving; his death would come by his sister's rage. His mouth hung open as Spupaleena continued to chew him out. He glanced around for his father to defend him, but somehow he had slipped away, probably hiding behind a tree, laughing in sheer delight.

He was sure the two of them had their attack plan all laid out, ready to pounce as soon as he came into sight, which they did. His punishment had only just begun.

Carmen Peone

Spupaleena finally took a breath, and Pekam was able to explain. "I only wanted to help. I knew you were worried about the upcoming race; you were torn between taking care of Elizabeth and training Dusty. I just wanted to help you like you always help everyone else." He felt beat but not defeated, not yet. He lifted his chin standing behind the truth of his explanation. It was sincere, and she had to see that.

Silence hung in the air, and for a split second, Pekam thought that was also planned. *Yes, let the boy tremble in his skin.* He was sure this all was a big set up. Spupaleena shifted her weight and folded her hands in front of her. She fingered the fringe on her doeskin dress.

"Pekam, lim lumt for your concern. Spupaleena scanned the boy in front of her. He was covered in dust. Strands of loose hair escaped from his braids and flopped in the breeze. "I know your heart is in the right place, but don't ever do that again. I can handle things. I had a plan. I have a plan, and if you would have stuck around, you would have seen that it included you."

Pekam hung his head. "I'm sorry," he said with firm conviction as if that were enough. He knew he failed his sister, which was the last thing he intended. He now cost her precious time.

"I believe you, but now you will have to do some chores first. When you're done, and I mean completely done with everything, you can start riding with me again."

Her words made him smile, and his eyes brightened. "What do I need to do first?" He felt a twinge of hope.

"Well, you need to eat. I doubt you packed much of anything."

He refrained from arguing. His body would require plenty of food to tackle the long list of repentance work, he was certain.

"I'll go over your chores when you're done eating. Some of us have added a few more to the list." At this point it was a challenge to keep a serious look on her face.

He sauntered over to where his family and the Gardners were almost ready to eat their noon meal. He went into his father's pit house to drop off his pack and overheard two men whispering.

One man he thought was Phillip, the other he was not quite sure. He could barely make out the gist of the conversation, only that Spupaleena would have to miss the next race. By the following one, Elizabeth would be in good enough shape for Spupaleena to feel like she could enter.

Pekam's mind instantly started reeling. He quickly forgot about his punishment. His adolescent brain could focus solely on the race. He would simply be taking Dusty for the day. Convincing himself was easy, but he could never persuade the others. He thought, *Kewa, I could do that. She never said I wasn't allowed to race him; by then, my chores will be done. She said I would be back in the saddle.* A satisfied smile emerged on his boyish face. He was now convicted that his plan was bulletproof. Yet he felt as if his insides were fighting and was puzzled as to why. He convinced himself that his actions were good, helpful, justified.

Three weeks later, his chores were complete. Spupaleena was busy with the Gardner children down by the river. She had planned to ride when the hot, dry air cooled off. The race she was opting out of was just up the river. Pekam pretended to brush Rainbow. He was really spying to see where his family was. Most everyone had gone down by the river to cool off. The coast was clear.

He snatched up Dusty's bridle, quickly and quietly placed his tack on, and scanned the area yet again. His conscience told him to stay put, but his will gave him permission to run the race, suggesting he could win. He led the colt out, tiptoeing just in case, and walked him to the tree line. Glancing back, he saw no one.

"Look, everyone, Spupaleena has her baby brother riding for her now!" one of the racers said, laughing. Some of them had painted faces. Most wore neatly braided hair and sat proudly on their mounts, attempting to convince the onlookers that they would be the pair to win.

"Yeah, she can't handle riding with the men." They all laughed and war-hooped. Their horses circled and danced about from all the commotion. Dust stirred in the blazing afternoon air.

Pekam remained silent although inside he was seething. The men slung tirades of insults at him. But Pekam sat quietly, chin up. He had ample time in prayer on the way over. He was confident that he could pull off this win. He needed it more than the others did. His sister's wrath flashed in his mind; that was enough to spur him into action.

Someone announced the time had come to line up. Pekam's blood rushed throughout his veins. All the sudden, he could hardly take in a breath. The reins felt slick with his sweat, yet his mouth was bone dry. His entire body trembled with fear, but he knew he could not come home empty. He could never return home empty. Glancing over at the mound of booty, his eyes grew wide. His sister would surely forgive him with a batch like that. He had to have it all. He had to take this win.

The horses continued to spin around, bumping one another as they attempted to form some kind of line. When they were close to horizontal, the starting cry echoed down the row of spectators. The crowd went wild, cheering and clapping as the wild-eyed horses careened down the path.

Dusty and Pekam were last but not far behind. Pekam had remembered to bring Spupaleena's crop and had watched her use it. He gently tapped the stallion on his rump and felt the power kick in. It only took light bumps, and his stride lengthened. Pekam could feel the colt reach with his forelegs. He felt the power underneath his legs. "Let's fly boy," he said under his breath.

Dusty dug into the grassy, dirt lane with all he had. They came up on each horse as if hardly any effort was put forth. Pekam reached back and walloped the horse, not realizing his strength, but the horse only ran harder for him. They were merely two horses away from the frontrunner and moving up swiftly. Pekam stretched his arms toward the colt's ears, put his chin into his chest, and hollered with all his might. Dusty felt the boy's will and put every ounce of strength he had into his being, crossing the finish rope a nose ahead of the rivaling horse.

A chill ran up Pekam's spine. He had never traveled that fast. His eyes were as big as his smile. He somehow managed to rein Dusty to a stop as the other horses sped past. He turned the colt around and began to walk him back. The crowd froze with astonishment, staring at the boy trying to make sense of what they had just witnessed. Then suddenly, they burst out cheering and patting Dusty as they rode past as if someone cued them. The colt pranced, holding his head and tail high.

Now Pekam knew how his sister felt when she won. "Lim lumt, Creator God," he hollered, waving his hand in the air. He would honor the God who allowed him this win.

Pekam made his way to his winnings. He glanced at the pile and wondered how he would get it all home. Out of nowhere, a tiny, elderly woman strolled over with a smaller, bay horse in tow. Her doeskin dress was adorned with meticulous bead work displaying floral hues of reds, greens, and purples. Her moccasins matched her dress. On her head sat a tightly woven basket hat. She carried her head high and confident. She looked up at Pekam and gestured for him to take the horse. "For me?" She nodded and walked away. *This day just gets better and better,* he thought. He packed his belongings on the mare and headed for home, fully grasping God's favor.

Chapter 12

"Where have you been?" Spupaleena hissed, marching up to the corral where Pekam was unsaddling her colt. She looked so angry, he thought her eyes would pop out of their sockets and slap him in the face. He wondered if he should just drop everything and run...fast. Instead he turned to her like the man he wished to be, shaking like a scared rabbit. He swallowed.

"I raced for you, and look at what I won. I thought you'd be happy." Pekam lowered his gaze. He fidgeted until his sister finally spoke. A million reasons to bolt reeled through his mind. Only seconds had passed, but it felt like days.

Spupaleena gasped and her eyes grew wide and blank. "You won? You rode Dusty and won? I-I can't believe it." She smiled and her anger dissipated. After a brief moment as the shock wore off, she patted her brother on the back. She laughed and then drew him

Carmen Peone

into a giant bear hug. She put him down and asked again if he had really won.

The boy nodded with the biggest and brightest smile on his face. His thoughts about running off were completely gone.

"Wow, I just can't believe it." She put her hand up to her forehead as she shook her head. "Nice job, but you're back in big trouble. You can't keep taking off and with my horse." She set her hands on her hips.

"I—"

"How'd he handle? How did you know what—" Her excitement sparked again.

"I watch you. I study your every move—how you ride with your hands and legs, how you sit in the saddle or ride bareback, when you urge him to run, even get him to travel faster, how you hold him back a little bit in the beginning of each race and then let him loose only to speed up, pass the others, and win." Pekam hopped around, pretending he was a galloping horse.

Spupaleena stood smiling, watching her brother's dramatic production. Once the adrenaline drained out of his system, Pekam bent over, panting. After a couple minutes, he stood upright, raising his hands over his head, twisting from side to side. Spupaleena leaned against a tree, crossing her arms and waiting for her brother's full attention. Finally, he looked her in the eyes and spoke.

"I'm sorry, Spupaleena. I want to race too, and I thought I would be helping you out." His face held a small pout.

"You are, but quit taking my horse." She bent forward and fluffed his long, straggly hair. He laughed and motioned to do the same to his forgiving sister, but she held her hand in front of him. "By the way, remember the chore list? Start over." She turned on her heels and strode away.

Pekam could care less about his repentance work; the look of pride reflected on his sister's face was plenty to keep him content for the rest of his life. He hopped around in circles, whooping and dancing around like a rooster on fire. His sister was proud, that was all he needed to hear.

Spupaleena smiled behind his back; she was more than proud. Inside, she felt like she could rupture. Her brother won on her stallion. *Way to go, sintahoos,* she thought.

"Is he back?" Skumhist asked as Spupaleena walked up. Her father sat in the shade of his tule-pit home. He was repairing his torn fishing net, telling stories with Phillip.

"Yeah, he's back. Went to the race."

"What?" Phillip said, lifting an eyebrow.

"He not only ran, he won." Spupaleena emphasized the win with her hands.

"On Dusty?" Skumhist asked, rubbing his hands down his braids. "My boy won?"

The three peered at one another in amazement and chuckled in disbelief. Phillip could only shake his head. Skumhist deliberated whether he should be proud of his son or make him do hard labor for the next several years.

Spupaleena looked at her father. "I told him to start over on his list of chores, which I caught him calling his repentance work." She snickered.

Skumhist nodded, holding out a cool drink for his daughter. "Good, I may add a few things as well." She took it and swallowed heartily. It was exhausting to be the punisher. She suddenly had a new respect for her father.

"I may need some clothing washed or something," Phillip added, smiling.

Pekam led his newly acquired pony over to where they stood, with his plunder hanging lopsided, and his smile so wide most of his teeth were exposed. "Look, mistum, I'll share with you—all of you." He motioned to the trio with his free hand.

They looked at one another and chuckled. Pekam was so sincere it was hard to be mad at him. They were just thankful he made it home safely. However, they all cheerfully added to his repentance work.

"Perhaps after your chores are done for today," Skumhist said, his voice trying not to sound too humorous.

"Kewa, I know, I'll get right to it. But first, can I show you what I won?"

Skumhist pondered his son's request. He took his time, letting the boy sweat a bit. Pekam could hardly stand still, his skin itched with eagerness until finally, his father agreed. He sighed and began to untie his booty. He relived the entire race for them play by play, acting out his role as well as the others. Skumhist noticed, for the first time, how truly proud of his son he really was.

"What's all the excitement about?" Elizabeth asked. She was so tired but welcomed a small amount of conversation. Simillkameen knew no English, and she was hungry for womanly exchange. Any amusing dialogue was appreciated. She was tired of being cooped up. Simillkameen anticipated Elizabeth's recovery would soon allow her to get up and around for spots at a time, but she had to remain on bed rest until then.

"Pekam thought he'd help me out and run today's race."

"You're kidding."

"Loot, he not only ran it, but he won."

Elizabeth chuckled. "You mad?"

She shook her head. "I know his heart is good, he so badly wants to help." She handed Elizabeth a cool cloth. "I was furious at first. But I know he's just trying to pull his own weight."

"He's got a heart of gold." Elizabeth sighed. She closed her eyes and patted her face and neck, soaking up the coolness on her hot, sticky skin.

"Kewa, I told him to stop running off, and now he has to do his chores all over again." Spupaleena giggled.

"Huh, I wonder who he got the idea to *run* off from?" Elizabeth grinned, glancing up at her friend.

Carmen Peone

Spupaleena gave her a sideways glance. "Yeah, I wonder." They both laughed. "Guess I need to be a better example."

"You are. Otherwise, he wouldn't want to follow your every footstep. He sure loves you, sister." Elizabeth handed the cloth back to her friend.

"I love him, too. Don't know what I'd do without him."

"I've been thinking," Elizabeth said. She glanced around the tule-pit home in search of her hair brush.

"About what?" Spupaleena dipped the cloth back into a bucket of creek water and wrung the excess out then handed it back to Elizabeth.

"You need to continue training. I'm fine, and your cousin said she would help with the children," Elizabeth said softly, holding the brush out.

Spupaleena took it and lowered her gaze to the dirt floor. After a moment, she scooted beside Elizabeth and started to brush her cascading blond tresses.

"I love having you around, but you need to ride. You need to live your dreams. I'm just fine, and the baby is strong. Nothing bad is going to happen. Simillkameen has taken wonderful care of me, okay?"

Spupaleena nodded. "I know. I do want to start riding again, I just…" Sadness and confusion swarmed her.

"I understand you wanting to care for me as I have to you, but look at me." Spupaleena lifted her eyes and peered at Elizabeth. "Nothing bad is going to happen. God has it all under control. Besides, I'm getting stronger every day." She took Spupaleena's hand in her own. "I wait quietly before God, for my victory comes from him. He alone is my rock and my salvation, my fortress where I will never be shaken."

Spupaleena nodded in agreement. "In the morning, I'll begin."

Elizabeth smiled. "Good. Now, what else can you tell me that will make me laugh? Tell me everything Pekam shared with you guys." Spupaleena returned to brushing her friend's thick hair.

The ladies had a chance to chitchat for a while before Simillkameen kicked out Spupaleena. She needed to check the baby and Elizabeth needed her rest. She was a staunch woman who took her healing duties seriously. Spupaleena had never seen the woman smile.

The warmth of the early morning air felt refreshing to Spupaleena. She loved the summer months, the cool river, the chorus of buzzing grasshoppers, and the chirping birds. She took in a deep breath and let it out slowly, glad Elizabeth talked her into riding. She took time to stretch her stiff muscles. She sat around too much these past few weeks. It was time to get back into shape so she could keep up with Dusty. She would need her strength to handle the brute.

She hoped to beat Pekam out of bed and have a quiet conversation with God before she began her day. The sound of dry leaves crunching under foot came from way of the corrals. She glanced over, and sure enough, he was up early. Her brother was committed to earning his trust back and was working hard on his demanding repentance list. But he toiled with a smile.

"Hey, lthkickha," he hollered, waving. Spupaleena waved back. She thought he would come after her, but apparently, he was serious about his responsibilities. She was impressed.

Spupaleena moseyed down to the river and found a quiet spot north of the village on a knoll overlooking the stunning sunrise reflecting off the water. The sky revealed soft pinks as the sun peeked over the mountains. She felt alive and peaceful all at the same time. She found a soft, grassy spot and sat down, praising God for Pekam's safety. She asked him for protection and perspective. She prayed for a clean heart and sound mind; for a focus so narrow she could never be side tracked by the enemy's tricks. After feeling fulfilled and settled, she sang gloriously, closing her eyes and lifting her hands to the heavens. She could feel the spirit of God envelope her, and she marveled in his presence.

It was midmorning when Jack rode up on Sampson, his giant black and white paint stallion. He wore a dark brown Stetson and tan chinks and sat tall and comfortable, like he'd been born in the saddle. The onlookers stared at the pair who radiated confidence and control. The children in the village stopped playing and stared at the valiant spectacle.

Jack smiled brightly as he spotted his friends. Skumhist had been teaching Phillip how to prepare hides the native way. They washed the slimy brain solution off their hands and stood to greet the rugged looking cowboy as he effortlessly dismounted his horse.

"How's Elizabeth?" The men greeted each other with a firm embrace.

Phillip nodded as he dried off his hands. "She's getting stronger by the minute. She'll be fine and so will the baby." He tossed the rag on a log to dry.

"What a relief. Good news, my friend." He turned to Skumhist. "You look well. How are you and your family? I see Pekam is hard at work." Jack motioned in the boy's direction.

Skumhist and Phillip exchanged glances and chuckled. They sat with a glass of cool water and enlightened Jack concerning Pekam's racing adventure. He was astonished and excited. He could see Pekam racing seriously in a few years. He had his sister's passion and athleticism. Even his balance was strong. All he needed was a batch of control.

"Where's Spup?" Jack asked, scanning the village.

"She should be back soon. She's back to riding now that Elizabeth's better."

"Good." Jack clapped his hands together. "I have something for her."

"What is it?" Skumhist asked, glancing at Phillip quizzically. Phillip shrugged; a broad smile on his face. He was thrilled, another surprise.

"Soon, my friends, soon enough." He fought to hide his enthusiasm but wanted Spupaleena to be the first to hear.

A short time elapsed before Spupaleena trotted up on her dripping wet, huffing horse. The trio stood and walked to where she ground–tied the colt. She unbuckled the cinch and tossed the saddle aside, and then picked two handfuls of grass and proceeded to rub the colt down.

Skumhist handed her a cold glass of water, and she took a long drink. The air was hot and dry, and her mouth was parched. The water was refreshing as it cascaded down her throat. She drank slowly to keep her head from hurting, which was difficult, as thirsty as she was.

Jack smiled, standing motionless, attempting to reveal nothing. He loved surprises.

"How are ya?" Spupaleena said, greeting him with a sweaty hug.

"Good, how are the workouts?" Jack smiled, keeping his focus on the colt.

"Great, he's getting stronger and faster if you can believe that." Spupaleena stared at the man. She had seen this face before and braced herself.

"Wow, faster? Didn't know he could get faster. That's great." Jack was overenthusiastic. He never was much at acting.

Spupaleena watched him closely. "Kewa. He's just great. I'm so happy with him, and he's got a pleasant mind. He's confident and smooth. Couldn't ask for a better horse." Spupaleena rubbed Dusty's nose as he nuzzled her, searching for a treat. "What brings you this far?"

Jack flashed the others a sideways glance and looked back at Spupaleena. She looked at everyone else. They all stood with their gazes' on Jack just as curious. "I'm glad you asked." He said smiling. "I brought Sampson over to cover Rainbow so you can start your own line."

Spupaleena stared at him like a stunned rabbit. The corners of her mouth turned up, and she took a step toward Jack.

"We're going to breed the two? For real?" She grabbed her braids.

"Yes, for real." Jack removed his Stetson and wiped the sweat from his brow.

"This has been my dream. Sampson, he's so glorious." Spupaleena ran her fingers down the length of her braids. She stood in shock, wordless, which was rare. Her mind encouraged her to take a few steps in his direction, but her body would not budge; she was too excited. She stood trembling as tears welled up in her big, black eyes. She was tired of crying. She shoved her emotions back down in the pit of her being and clapped her hands.

"Congratulations, Spup," Phillip said, patting her back.

Skumhist hugged his daughter. "This will be a good start to your herd, stumpkeelt. I'm proud of you."

Spupaleena looked at her father. *I'm proud of you.* She embraced her father again and just held him for a moment. Those few simple words were what she longed to hear. Skumhist released his hold on her and let the others get in their congratulatory hugs.

"Later on, we'll introduce the two and let 'em get acquainted," Jack said. He was thrilled Spupaleena was so happy. He was sure his stallion would produce quality offspring that would bring her a good price for the foals; the beginning of her own beautiful line.

Rainbow would be a good match with her head, revealing a nice shape and having spectacular balance. Her shoulder sloped long and angular, allowing for a longer stride. Her back was short with a long underline. Her neck was trim and refined. Sampson had big, coal eyes, and when he gazed at someone, he communicated willingness and confidence flavored with a sense of camaraderie.

Combined with Sampson's muscular build and gentle manner, they would be the perfect pair. His splash of color would be the finishing touch to a dazzling baby. Eleven months would be a long wait for a youngster, yet being born in the summer may not be a bad plan. Spupaleena would have time to get a good start on spring training before the foal came. It would be ideal.

Later that night, everyone was sitting outside enjoying the coolness of the evening. A gentle breeze drifted off the river under a carpet of twinkling stars that brightly lit the night. The lucid moon glowed in its fullness. Pekam almost hated to spoil the festive mood with cold-hearted innuendos. But he figured his feisty sister would want to know what others were saying.

He sat for a few minutes and thought long and hard about saying anything. His frazzled nerves could no longer bear the secret. He tried to swallow, but his mouth was too dry. His palms sweat, and his heartbeat began to race. He glanced at her, over to his father, and back to his sister. He blinked. Noticing he was holding his breath, Pekam let it rush out his gaping mouth.

"Spupaleena…" Her name came out in a high–pitched, squeaking sound. He was mortified.

"What is it, Pekam? You look like you just lost your best friend. What's the matter?"

The boy suddenly felt everyone's eyes fixed on him. He was glad the darkness masked his flame-red face. His stomach felt like a dull knife scraped the lining. *Why does this bother me so much?* he thought. He now wondered if he should have just kept his mouth shut.

"I...I..." He looked down at his trembling hands.

Everyone patiently waited while he tried to gather his thoughts and his courage.

"The other riders taunted me when I raced the other day. They were asking me if I was racing because you were too scared and asked if you finally figured out what woman's work was. They said you should stay away and let the real men race and that you should stay home and cook and..." He wiped his face with the crook of his arm, nearly in tears from the intense hatred bubbling deep inside. But he was also relieved to speak the words out loud.

"And what, Pekam?" Spupaleena already knew that she had been gossiped about behind her back. Her heart sank for her brother to have to endure the ridicules that belonged to her.

"They said you should find a man...and..." He gazed at his sister with devoted eyes. "They would be more than willing to...you know."

"Stop! You don't need to tell me anymore." She darted from the log she sat on, moving to her brother. She took his hand in hers.

"Hahoola<u>who</u> was there watching, and he said terrible things—"

"Hahoola<u>who</u> is a coward! Don't worry about what he says. He'll get what's coming to him, you'll see."

Spupaleena stood, picking up a nearby stick and tossing it into the fire, flinging sparks in all directions. Everyone scrambled out of the way. She turned to leave, but Skumhist caught her arm. "Sit down, stump<u>k</u>eelt. We need to let go of foolish talk. Don't let it determine your path."

"He's right, we need to pray about it and let God vindicate for us," Phillip said.

The group sat in a circle and held hands. They asked the Creator to forgive those who mocked Spupaleena and Pekam. They prayed for wisdom and guidance and for Pekam to have peace and to avoid Satan's traps. They prayed for the other riders and their malicious attitudes.

The enemy had no hold over them, and with Jesus fighting on their behalf, they would remain safe and strong. They would unite in prayer and petition, imploring the Holy Spirit to touch the hearts of the racers, as well as their own.

Chapter 13

"Come on, sintahoos; get that pony of yours goin'. You're slower than a snail in winter." Spupaleena flashed her brother a teasing grin.

"You watch out, I'll be winning more races than you could ever dream about." Pekam felt unbeatable, especially now that he no longer had the weight of the secret lugging him down.

After praying the night before, Pekam had a renewed peace and joy that he desperately needed. He hated being wound up in another's scandalous behavior. It was freeing to drop the oppressive attitude coming against him. Pekam recognized the spiritual fight within him and knew the strength of prayer. He looked forward to his youthful growth—not only physically and emotionally, but spiritually. He wanted to mature and be a strong leader as he saw his father becoming.

"I'm going to gallop him for a few miles, so why don't you keep working *Taka Takum* ("Thunder") through the trees? He's getting softer. You both look good."

"Lim lumt," Pekam said through an ear-to-ear grin. He ate up his sister's compliments. The more she offered, the more confident he became. He was thankful for a sister who was encouraging and not demeaning. He was also thankful for his new pony, a perfect fit. He loved his stocky build and round, dark eyes. They were soft and willing. He had long straight legs for a small horse, and a larger-than-life personality to go with his courageous spirit.

Spupaleena whirled Dusty around and took off down the trail. She could feel his desire to take the reins away from her, but Spupaleena kept him in check. He was feeling great and so was she. The sun was low and the air still. They liked to work the horses before the blistering afternoon heat settled in for the day.

The pair was in a nice rhythm until Spupaleena's thoughts wandered into stormy territory. She could visualize Hahoolawho's twisted face as he taunted her and Pekam. His hateful, dark eyes bored into her. She could handle his blatant remarks, but under no terms would he gain permission to mess with her brother. Her mind rambled on as she fought off the mental attacks. Spupaleena would show the world she could handle herself if she had to and convey the fact that Pekam was off limits.

"It takes a *man* to pick on a boy," she seethed.

Just then, she was catapulted forward, hitting her stomach on the saddle horn. Groaning, she caught her breath. Dusty darted all over the trail, still galloping, and stumbled as his right front hoof sunk in a gopher hole. He whinnied and fell to his knees. Spupaleena lost her balance and flew out of the saddle and into a pile of jagged rocks.

She lay on the hard ground, stunned but unhurt. Her arms were scraped, but nothing bandaging would not fix. Her eyes searched for her colt, finding him sprawled out on his side and gasping for air. She rolled over and scrambled to his side.

"You okay, boy?" She stroked his neck and talked softly to him. "I'm so sorry. I should have kept my mind on you, not…" She refused to speak his name. Nestling her face in his mane, she wept for her selfishness. "I'm sorry, God; forgive me for not trusting you to take care of my enemies. Forgive my poisoned thoughts; help me keep my mind on your goodness."

Dusty whinnied and rocked himself into a sitting position. Spupaleena got a closer look at his bloody knees. There was no time for self-pity. She coaxed him up and asked him to take a step forward. He limped, attempting to take a couple of quick steps, and shook his head, groaning deeply. He stood, afraid to take another painful step.

She ran her hands down Dusty's legs and ankles. There was heat. There was damage. Guilt quickly consumed her. She fought off the hot tears threatening to spill down her cheeks. Spupaleena remembered finding a stream not too far off when she was younger. If she could get him there and soak his legs, they could make it home.

Hastily, but cautiously, she led Dusty a short way. They had to pick their way down a brushy hill to get there, but it would be worth it. Once they were past the underbrush, a grassy bank came into view. Just down from there was a sandy area, perfect for leading the animal into the belly-deep water.

Spupaleena hurriedly unlaced her moccasins and tossed them aside. She took off her buckskin breeches and waded out in her knee-length doeskin dress. Even after sewing the cotton dress with Elizabeth, she preferred her traditional outfits, adding pants to ride in. They held up better when she brushed up against the thorns and underbrush.

Dusty willingly followed her into the cool water and stood quietly. He was now breathing normal and drank in a mouthful of clear water. Spupaleena stared at the sparkling droplets dripping from nearby leaves into a small pool nestled on the side of the creek. A thought rushed into her head: the next race or two would be out of the question, for Dusty, anyhow. He was too special to tax his banged up body. She would have to find a suitable mount to ride until the colt recovered. Jack would surely have something, and there was no way she was backing out of another race.

As she waited for the swelling to recede, Spupaleena reflected on the condition of her heart. She prayed for understanding. Since emotions were unpredictable, she had to search for that fine line of taking action the Lord would expect of her opposed to knowing when to step aside, allowing God to do his own bidding. It was confusing to her. Her heart said keep going, but her mind kept playing the same old tune: *give up, it's too hard, too much work. Everyone is against you…laughing at you…give up.*

Spupaleena shook her head and cleared her thoughts. "God, please lead me down the trail you want me to go, please make it clear." She leaned into Dusty's neck and rubbed his nose as a tear slipped down her cheek. He nuzzled her as if to comfort her, letting her know he would heal, and they would ride again soon.

"What're you going to do now?" Pekam asked. His face and drooped shoulders displayed his discouragement. He felt so bad for his sister, but at the same time was glad it was not his own fault.

"I'm trying to figure out if Jack has a horse he could lend me for a few races." Spupaleena did her best to smile and hide her own displeasure.

"I have a four-year-old Appy," Jack interjected as he came into view from the shadow of the lean-to.

Spupaleena spun around and faced him. "You do?" The look on her face revealed her relief.

"Yes, I do. She'll get you through a race or two until Dusty recovers. She'll work well for you. She's strong and willing. She may not win but will hold her own."

"Jack, lim lumt." Spupaleena felt an enormous heaviness lifted off her. She let out a deep sigh, feeling her body relax.

"You're welcome." Jack put his broad hand on her slim shoulder. "Dusty'll be okay. Elizabeth knows some herbs that will get him up to speed in a short time. Pekam can take him to stand in the water multiple times a day too." Jack looked at the boy who hastily agreed.

"I can help however you want." Pekam nodded his head eagerly.

"You both are…" Spupaleena glanced at the pair.

"We know," Pekam said as he gave his sister a poke in the stomach. He bounced away in his usual manner.

Jack chuckled as he watched the boy leave, shaking his head and then grew serious. "It's only a couple of races." He nodded and looked her in the eyes.

Spupaleena looked up at him. "I know," she whispered through disheartenment.

Jack tipped his Stetson. "I better hit the trail so I can get that mare to you bright and early." Spupaleena thanked him and went to check on Dusty, thanking God as she walked.

Jack saddled up quickly and rode home. He turned around at the crack of dawn the following morning, leading the mare behind.

In the meantime, Spupaleena, Skumhist, and Pekam set out to make a portable corral, one strong enough to keep a stallion at bay. She would need to be able to rotate Dusty in order to graze yet keep quiet so his leg would heal. The cool water he soaked in would be his main therapy. Between Elizabeth and Simillḵameen, they would have the perfect herbal concoction.

It was late morning when Jack arrived. The Appaloosa mare appeared strong and big but almost too bulky. She would be good with cows and short spins and sprints but not the longer races Spupaleena was accustomed to. If Jack were correct, her heart would be the winning factor. She would make up for her lack of endurance with sheer grit.

Spupaleena eyed her as Jack rode up. She had a pleasing look to her and a soft, feminine head. Her chocolate coat and flowing black mane and tail shone in the sun. Her rump was covered with a white blanket that was peppered with brown spots. She carried herself with assurance and courage.

"Her name's Delilah." Jack smirked. How appropriate. She was a beautiful, promising, young mare.

Spupaleena smiled up at Jack. "I like her; she should work out just fine."

Jack nodded. "Where do you want her?"

"Here, I'll take her." Spupaleena reached for the lead rope, and Jack let it slide out of his grip.

"Hey, girl," she whispered. "We'll get along just fine." Spupaleena rubbed her hand down Delilah's back and through her sleek, thick tail. She walked around the mare, checking over every inch of her bulky, straight body. She smiled in satisfaction. Jack always seemed to pull through, and with the finest of God's creatures.

"Why don't you toss a saddle on, and let's take her out before lunch."

Spupaleena nodded, taking Delilah to go and saddle up.

They rode for quite a while as Spupaleena and Delilah became familiar with one another. Spupaleena knew the minute she sat in the saddle they would be a good match. The mare felt like a hand in a glove.

Spupaleena figured they could do better than somewhere in the middle, as Jack put it. Delilah had a heart of courage, and her rider knew it. Spupaleena was determined to fight for the chance to beat Hahoolawho. She could see herself nose to nose and pulling ahead to cross the line first. She imagined the look on his face when she won, his ugly, twisted face. She smiled at the thought.

She felt a nudge letting her know this attitude was not honoring to herself or God. The smile quickly faded. Sighing, she swapped the hideous thoughts for the work before her. Two weeks would be plenty of time to prepare.

Jack, as usual, already had a great start on the mare, and her job would be easy. She was soft and easygoing. Spupaleena would merely need to introduce her to more obstacles at a faster pace. There was no doubt Delilah could handle anything Spupaleena put in front of her.

Jack, Spupaleena, and their mounts negotiated the trees, circling as many as they could, avoiding the leg-high brush and jumping over downed logs. They picked their way up and down steep hills, giving Spupaleena a chance to get a good feel for the mare.

When the horses' sides were heaving, they finally slowed their pace and headed home.

Watch out, Hahoolawho, we're coming to get you!

Chapter 14

"Hey, little boy, you here to lead your sister's horse or ride for her?" A boyish voice assaulted him from the distant trees, obviously not brave enough to say anything to one's face.

Pekam held his tongue. Fury engulfed him, but he knew restraint was the answer. He said a little prayer in order to keep his cool.

"Look, Spupaleena's servant boy!" The surrounding youth stood, gawking and laughing. Pekam walked on, gritting his teeth. He clenched his fists, glaring at the ground. Delilah whinnied and danced around, feeling the electricity running throughout the crowd. The whites of her eyes showed, and her nostrils flared. This was the first time the poor girl had been around so many high-strung horses and such a high-energy crowd. She began to tremble and perspire. Spupaleena began to doubt if the mare could handle the pressure.

A young boy jumped in front of Pekam and shoved him. He tripped to the side but managed to regain his footing. He looked at the scrappy-haired boy blocking his path. The bully stared into Pekam's eyes, looking tough and ready to fight. Pekam had never seen him before nor understood why he was challenging him. Delilah halted and stood with her ears forward and focused on the scuffle, which took her attention off her anxiety.

"What do you want?" Pekam asked. He tried to keep his voice calm yet courageous. He tried his best to honor God.

"We asked you a question, and you need to answer it." The boy stared him down. He was at least an inch taller than Pekam, twenty pounds heavier, and mean-looking. A scar ran down the middle of his cheek. His eyes were cold and looked like he could shoot arrows out of them. Dirt covered most of his skin and clothing, and he smelled just as rancid.

Pekam tried to walk around him, but the boy grabbed his arm. Pekam punched him in the stomach. The boy moaned and jumped on Pekam. They fell to the ground with a thud and rolled around with fists grazing anything in reach. Delilah skirted to the side, but kept her eyes and ears pinned on the boys.

Grabbing a hold of the boy's hair Pekam was able to flip him on his back and pin him to the ground. The boy's face pressed into the dirt.

"I'm here to help my lthkickha. She'll win this race, you wait and see!" Pekam straddled the boy and pushed himself up. Wiping the dust off his deerskin leggings, he reached for Delilah's reins. A young girl handed him the lead rope. She looked at him and grinned with admiration. Pekam gave her a small, awkward smile.

"Someone needed to stand up to him," she mumbled.

Pekam grunted and walked off.

The boy rolled over and sat up. He was dazed, ashamed to have been thumped by someone smaller and lighter. Pekam was much stronger and quicker than was predicted. In all his humiliation, the boy put his head in his hands and sat on the ground in defeat.

Pekam knew he had the right to defend himself. He felt light and somewhat grown up sticking up for his newfound values. He was proud of the God he now served and desired to honor him. That was the most controlled he had ever been in his life—all eleven years.

Approaching Spupaleena, she glanced at him with a questioning look. "I'll tell you later," Pekam sputtered. He shoved the lead into her hands and went to wash the blood off his face and arms. It wasn't much, a couple of scrapes was all, but he wanted to look presentable for the race. He wanted to feel good and refreshed while cheering on his sister. He even took the time to re-braid his hair.

Spupaleena watched his back as he marched off. Something was different. She failed to pinpoint it but would ask him about it later. She placed her hands on the mare and prayed for their safety. She prayed not for a win but simply to do their best and let the mare give her all.

She swung up on the saddle and with little effort asked the mare to walk to the start line. Pekam quickly caught up and walked by their side. They both looked straight ahead, confident, devoid of the slightest trace of arrogance.

Hahoola<u>who</u> caught sight of Spupaleena and sneered at her. She saw him out of the corner of her eye but refused to acknowledge his presence. She smiled inwardly and asked the Creator to keep her focused on her riding and not the evil being the enemy was using to propel her off balance.

She willed her eyes to look ahead. She spoke softly to Delilah, encouraging her to relax. Spupaleena drew in a deep breath and let it out as she sank deep in the saddle. She secured her feet into the stirrups and placed her hand on the mare's neck briefly to let her know she was ready.

Spupaleena could feel Hahoola<u>who</u>'s glowering eyes on her, but she shook it off. She was amused that he was threatened by her. If he was not bothered, he would have merely ignored her. But his attention seemed to be focused entirely on diminishing her chances of winning. His tactics were immature at best.

The start cry sounded, and they leaped into motion. Having not raced the horse before, Spupaleena was unsure how she would come off the line, but Delilah never balked. She thrust herself forward with all she had, nearly driving Spupaleena into the fork of the saddle and onto the mare's neck.

Spupaleena regained her composure and leaned her hands forward so Delilah was free to grab hold and dig in. The power in her hindquarters was remarkable. The question was if her staying power would in fact last to the end. Spupaleena held her steady until the last several yards then dug her heels in and urged the mare to reach forward. She reached back, tapping the mare's hind end with her whip, and Delilah gave her all.

Quiy S<u>k</u>et was a nose length ahead of Delilah when they crossed the finish rope, and Hahoola<u>who</u> was spitting-nails-mad they were that close. He glared back at Spupaleena, wanting to stick her with an arrow if he had one.

Spupaleena reined in the mare and circled her around. The crowd cheered not for Hahoola<u>who</u>'s win but Spupaleena's heart of courage. No woman had ever dreamed of racing, let alone having her amount of success. She never imagined they would be neck in neck, especially with Delilah, a short, stocky mare. Rubbing the mare's mane, she lifted her whip in the air and let out a whoop that echoed through the mountains. Jack was right, the gal had grit.

"Thank you, Creator God!" she shouted. "I give you the glory." Spupaleena rubbed the mare on her neck, smiling brightly.

Pekam trotted up to her hollering his praises to his sister and their God. Spupaleena swung her leg over to one side and slid off.

As brother and sister celebrated the success, Hahoola<u>who</u> galloped up and slid Quiy S<u>k</u>et to a stop, almost crashing into Delilah. He barked vulgar wishes at them, whirled around, and sped off in a huff. Spupaleena stepped in front of her brother in a protective manner.

Pekam peered up at his sister, unsure of how to react. Inside, he wanted to grab the wicked snake and jerk him off his horse. Instead, he shrugged his shoulders and proceeded to lift Spupaleena's arm into the air and cheered some more. They laughed and danced around and hugged those who greeted them, which felt much more uplifting than seeking revenge.

There would be no prizes to gather, but Spupaleena cared less. Her satisfaction came in the form of respect and honor. Something her opponent lacked. She would later have to ask Jack about purchasing Delilah, who she now had a deep love and respect for. She would not only be a good working horse, but perhaps a good kids' horse. Or better yet, a trusty mount for her father. She snickered at the thought of her father learning to ride, if it was even possible.

Spupaleena ran two other races with Delilah. She came in second once more against Hahoolawho and won the race he opted out. Apparently, in one of Hahoolawho's raging fits, he managed to somehow injure his ribs and was unable to participate. Only God knows what the fool was doing.

However, his injury could possibly give Spupaleena the advantage. Hahoolawho's pride disallowed anyone else to ride his stallion. The week off could prove detrimental; nonetheless, Quiy Sket was so puissant, time off could give him enough respite to come back more forceful than ever. That was a risk she had to take.

Dusty was gaining strength. Jack had been riding him the past week, and the stud colt was gaining momentum rapidly. His swelling was completely gone, and his stamina was improving. He was almost up to speed. Spupaleena was anxious to get him back on track. But patience would pay off. He needed to be in top shape before she would race him again, better than he last ran, especially if she had any chance of beating Quiy S<u>k</u>et.

Chapter 15

"Spupaleena, I want to talk to you," Skumhist announced. "Come on, let's go for a walk."

She nodded and followed his lead. They walked to the river and headed south. They walked in silence for a long time until Skumhist turned to face his daughter and reached for her hands.

Spupaleena felt confused. He had been acting secretive lately, but she decided not to make too much of it. She had put her energy into preparing for the final upcoming race.

"Let's sit." He motioned to a log beside the river. They settled into a comfortable position, and Spupaleena waited for her father to speak. She placed her bare feet into the water and swirled them around, enjoying the coolness.

"I thought I knew your God, but after visiting many days with Phillip, I discovered I don't know him like I desire or should."

Spupaleena nodded. She remained silent so her father could say all he needed to without interruption. Skumhist picked up a small rock and flung it into the current. Spupaleena swallowed hard.

"I want to pray with you…I want *you* to lead me to the Creator and his son." Skumhist's eyes reflected a tenderness she had never known before. "Will you pray with me?"

Spupaleena nodded. Her body trembled with such a thrill. She glanced to the heavens in praise and fulfillment. "Kewa," she whispered, drawing her gaze back to her father.

Squeezing his hands tightly, she led Skumhist in a prayer of repentance and acceptance. The gift of eternal life with Jesus was the ultimate prize—the one true crown worthy of exaltation. Spupaleena and Skumhist wept and prayed further together in worship. They took the rest of the afternoon to pour out their hearts to each other, revealing every attitude and feeling as honestly as possible.

After some time, they walked back and announced Skumhist's newly made commitment to the Gardners, Jack, and Pekam. A new type of pride shone on Skumhist's face. They celebrated amid other family members who shared the faith with a feast, singing and dancing into the night. Elizabeth was elated to be able to sit comfortably outdoors and rejoice with the others. She clapped her hands and sang with a revitalized passion. Phillip perched next to her with one child on each knee.

The next morning, Skumhist approached his daughter with a new perspective on the "lazy beasts". He rubbed his hands together. "What can I do to help?" He looked at the saddle and bridle laying in the grass, clueless as to how it all worked.

Spupaleena was taken back. She had no idea how he could help, never having been around the horses. She beamed inwardly, but her face remained emotionless. She dared not tease her father and scare him off. "I'm not sure, but we can figure something out." She smiled brightly at her father. Knowing he not only accepted her racing, but offered to take a part in the affair warmed her being from head to heels.

"Dusty's ready for a trial run," Jack said. He handed Spupaleena the reins. "He's sound and galloping smoothly. I have yet to let him go full out, thought I'd leave that to you." Jack winked at her. He stood, confident and eager. Spupaleena glanced at him. She had a hard time understanding why his clothing hung so neatly off his towering frame when he was about to sweat profusely. The heat of the morning was already reaching a record high.

"Good. I'm ready to take him out. Are you coming with us?" Spupaleena held out a carrot for the horse.

"Where you taking him?"

"I'm thinking of heading up river to the flats. It makes for a good grassy stretch. You can be my finish point." Spupaleena smiled.

"Be happy too." He tipped his Stetson.

"In fact, let's get a few others and see how he does. Where's Pekam?" Spupaleena glanced around and saw him sending his pony over some mini jumps he had recently made.

She hollered at him to round up some others, including himself, and meet her and Jack at the corral as quickly as they could.

In a matter of minutes, a bunch of scrawny, rambunctious boys and their well-fed ponies were lined up, trying to oust the other off their mounts. Jack and Spupaleena exchanged looks.

"This should be fun," Spupaleena mouthed to Jack.

Jack merely smiled and shook his head with an understanding grin. Spupaleena filled the youth in on the arrangement and the location of their destination. She spoke quickly as their attention span was as short as a clap of her whip.

"Okay, let's go," Spupaleena said with a tone of authority. The boys tore off shouting and laughing. They seemed to be thrilled that they were chosen. Whether they realized they would wear their ponies out before the practice race, she would never know.

Dusty pranced and threw his head from side to side, wanting to catch up to the sinewy group ahead, but Spupaleena wanted him as quiet as possible. She moved him in diagonals, circles, and side-passes attempting to keep his mind busy. Time off and green, river grass only made Dusty's adrenaline run as wild as a chipmunk chasing sunflower seeds.

Jack rode Sampson, keeping his stallion at a distance from Spupaleena's young colt. Sampson had never raced before and watched Dusty as if to ask what he was so hyped up over. He was all about relaxing and conserving energy for the day-long cattle duties. Dusty had enough get-up-and-go for them both.

They reached the grassy flats in a short time. The ponies were already covered in sweat, and so were their riders. The sky was cluttered with non-threatening gray clouds, and a breeze swept gently off the river, making for a wondrous ride.

After giving the tired horses a rest and a drink from a nearby creek, they all lined up. Jack held a flag, made from an old shirt tied on a stick, over his head. Once all eyes were locked on him, he dropped his arm, and the flag came down.

Spupaleena purposely held the colt back to give the boys a thrill then urged him forward when they were a few lengths ahead. Dusty was so fresh she hardly had to do much but hang on. He sped up, passing the pounding hooves of the other horses like they were on a Sunday trot. Dusty barely broke a sweat. He was more vigorous than Spupaleena had anticipated.

Jack smiled as she passed in front of him. "He's back," he mumbled, sitting up a might taller in the saddle, smiling brightly. He held the flag in the air, waving it wildly, letting out a loud, long howl.

The boys finally sped past, yelping their high-pitched war hoops. They roared with laughter. Everyone headed back to the creek for a quick gulp of water before going back to the village. The boys splashed about cooling off. Jack and Spupaleena willingly joined in the fun as the chilled water felt refreshing in the blistering heat.

They made their way back to the village in good time. The boys rode ahead, leaving Jack and Spupaleena time to visit about the upcoming race. Hahoola<u>who</u> would be there, and his stallion would be in top shape. They discussed and came up with a training schedule. She had two short weeks before the race and would need every minute to prepare.

After the evening meal, Spupaleena checked on Elizabeth. They caught up with one another, and she played with the Gardner kids before grabbing her packed bag. She was heading out to the corral when Skumhist caught her attention.

"Here's some extra moose meat for the ride home. Remember, you have to keep up your strength," he said. He placed his hands on her shoulders and met her gaze. "I will be praying for you stump<u>k</u>eelt. I know this race is important to you. Remember who you ride for."

She held his stare a little longer and nodded. "Kewa, I ride for God and God alone." They hugged, and she turned to go and fetch Dusty. She jumped up, swinging her leg over the colt's bare back effortlessly. Skumhist admired her athletic ability. She had always been light on her feet.

Spupaleena rode into the mountains to pray, fast, and train. She knew if she were to have any likelihood of beating Hahoola<u>who</u>, she would have to focus on nothing else but riding…and God.

Chapter 16

The time had come. The sun beat down on the crowd, and the rumbling of excitement waved up and down the multitude. The betting had begun far before breakfast. The contestants had not arrived to the start line yet. No clouds were seen, only the waves of heat rising off the desolate dirt. A breeze to relieve the scorching heat would at least be rejuvenating.

The tension was heaping high and fast. A race this electrifying had never existed. The crowd shouted who their victors would be, and most of them shouted the names of Hahoolawho and Spupaleena. No one else came close. They were in a rank of their own. The course and adjoining hills were lined with anxious bodies of bystanders. Children ran and played close to their mothers, mimicking their favorite racers.

There was a low rumble in the crowd as the first racer appeared. A shrilling cry sounded, and another rider emerged. More cries echoed in the distance as several racers materialized. The horses spun and pawed anticipating the rush of energy radiating not only from their rider but also the surrounding crowd pushing in on them. They knew what was to come. They knew in a short time that their hearts would be pounding and their hooves would strike the earth with fierceness. Each horse would give their heart as they tore down the lane. They were bred to run.

Spupaleena stood off in the shade of several towering aspen trees. Her friends and family surrounded her and Dusty. They gathered in a semicircle, laying their hands on the rider and her companion, praying for safety and honor. She felt the nasty stares hurled at her from the opposition. Her skin crawled as the image of Hahoolawho assaulted her mind. However, the longer they prayed, the more tranquil her spirit became. She held her braids tightly as she was bowing her head in prayer. Power came through the hands she felt on her head and back.

Spupaleena knew what she had to do. She knew who she had to glorify. Any dangling sense of intimidation galloped off, and a sense of strength and courage engulfed her. Surrender freed her to ride as God intended.

She was still nervous though because this race was different. It was more than a straight stretch on the cushion of soft grass. It was a seven-mile race up and down jagged hills, crossing fallen logs and debris, tearing through underbrush and finally crossing the Columbia River, scrambling up the bank and fighting to cross the finish rope, claiming the winning title.

It was time.

Pekam led the stud colt out for her as she walked behind. Dusty pricked his ears forward but remained calm and focused, his greatest attribute. He caught sight of Quiy Sket, and the two stallions seemed to lock gazes. Dusty never wavered; he was far from intimidation even though his opposition *was* twice his age.

As Spupaleena approached, the crowd went wild. Shouts of admonition and admiration began to roar. Some gave her pats of encouragement while others spat on her. She ignored it all and concentrated on whom she was to glorify; who she rode for. She would keep her eyes upon the Lord and let him take care of the rest. Someone hollered in the distance and it caught her attention. A man with three-fingered, red stripes across one cheek waved a fist at her, hurling insults. His long hair hung loose and straggly. Spupaleena stared expressionless. She felt nothing but the peace of God.

Looking to the side, she saw the other horses and riders scattered about the starting area. Red hand prints, green arrows, and blue lightning bolts were some of what were stamped on the horses' rumps. Spupaleena smiled, her eyes level with the horizon. She was content with her choice of three crosses lining Dusty's neck with three feathers tied down his mane.

Spupaleena finally came and stood face-to-face with the evil snake. Her eyes were fixed on his as he crept closer until they were mere inches apart. She refused to fall for his intimidating tactics. Catching a whiff of the putrid stench pulsating from his body, she nearly gagged. She wanted to vomit but swallowed hard instead. Everything about him reeked.

"You should be in the mountains picking berries with the rest of the women," Hahoola<u>who</u> said, glaring at Spupaleena. He spoke through clenched teeth as if it made him tougher.

"I will ride today—"

"With what? That broken-down animal won't get you far." Hahoola<u>who</u> laughed, searching the onlookers for support. A few whooped and laughed. Most turned their eyes to Spupaleena, silently waiting, eager for a reply.

"I ride for God—"

"God? You must show me this God of yours. Is he here?" Hahoola<u>who</u> interrupted. He turned from side to side with his hand shading his eyes, acting like he was looking for someone.

"Kewa, he's here. You'll see!" Spupaleena clutched the rein in her hand a little tighter and leaned forward. "I ride for him, you fool. You ride for yourself, and you will find yourself looking at Dusty's tail today."

Hahoola<u>who</u> slapped his leg and laughed, carrying on like someone who had stolen and drank some of Simill<u>k</u>ameen's herbs. Spupaleena forced herself to hold her tongue and keep from saying what was really in her mind. *Honor God*, she thought. Something unexplained came over Spupaleena, and she glanced at the crazy boy before her and instantly exploded with laughter. She felt the prayer coverage of those who interceded on her behalf.

This only fueled his already raging anger. "You're the foolish one, Spupaleena. Whatever made you think you could beat me?"

"Not what, but who." Spupaleena managed to stop giggling. She turned to walk off, and Hahoola<u>who</u> grabbed her arm. "Let go!" She tried to pull away, but his grasp tightened.

"You think you're so great, let's do this without saddles—just us and our stallions."

Spupaleena grinned and slowly nodded. She had been riding bareback all summer, and her balance was superb. She wrenched her arm away from his grasp and walked to Dusty. Pekam handed her the bridle with a grin and a nod. He unsaddled the colt and handed it off to Jack, who had watched the whole scene unfold. Jack snickered, almost pitying the boy. He believed Spupaleena would win this contest based on sheer determination. The boy had no idea what he was up against, Jack was sure.

"You have this, <u>lth</u>kickha," Pekam said quietly. He patted her leg and stepped aside. He didn't want to chance getting run over again.

"Spupaleena, winner takes all, including both stallions," Hahoola<u>who</u> barked.

Spupaleena's heart about stopped as doubt engulfed her. *Lord, help, what do I tell him?* she prayed. She closed her eyes and took in a deep, long breath and let it out slowly. She opened her eyes and looked at him, nodding. "It's done."

The crowd's zeal kicked into gear and individuals started tossing down hides, saddles, blankets, and more as the betting picked up where it left off. With each item added to the mound, the stakes gained in value. Spupaleena trembled with excitement. She could feel the adrenaline rush throughout her body, and her flesh burned like it was on fire.

Her eyes grew big as the booty piled high. Dusty pranced around as the electricity buzzed around the crowd like a lightning storm. Spupaleena closed her eyes and again prayed silently. *Lord, I ride for you and you alone. Show me your strength. Show me your confidence. Show me your will.* She drew in a breath, fully expanding her lungs, expelling the air slowly and deliberately. She wanted to stay focused on riding and not all the eye-catching goods before her.

She glanced sideways and saw Hahoola<u>who</u>'s pile was not as big as hers. She lifted her eyes and saw that he was glaring at her. She quickly lowered her eyes and stared at Dusty's mane. Her thoughts ran wild. Would he lose confidence and blow the race? Would his stallion pick up on his raw mood and fail to run as hard? *Focus!*

Reining in her whirling mind, Spupaleena searched the crowd for her family and friends. She saw her father beaming like a new daddy holding his baby for the first time. Her eyes traveled upward and caught sight of Phillip and Elizabeth watching her in what felt like a protective manner. They were sitting on a knoll with the kids, and she saw them wave. Pacing behind them was Jack. She lifted her chin and smiled. She had never seen him that intense.

She heard chanting nearby. Straining to hear what was being said, she caught her breath, hearing her own name. She craned her neck to the side and saw her extended family members waving and cheering. She gathered her courage and smiled brightly with all the support surrounding her.

Doubt departed and so did any ill will of her opponents, one in particular.

A distant birdlike whistle echoed in the hills, and she knew it was time to line up. She stroked Dusty's neck and mane, encouraging him to settle himself as he continued to whirl around, stomping and dancing with his forelegs. She prayed under her breath, soothingly stroking the colt's neck. Dusty continued jigging so she did the only thing she could think of: sing a lullaby. He turned his ears backward and listened to her soft voice, settling his feet.

The riders did their best to line up in some form of a horizontal row, ten in all. They could hardly contain the horses. Some whirled around, crashing into others. They whinnied and grunted as the riders tried to hold them straight.

Spupaleena was on the outside of the string to the right. She glanced down the line and saw Hahoolawho mouth offensive words to her. She smiled and winked at him. Spupaleena was sure she saw steam rolling out of his ears. Staring forward, she pinned her focus at a tree in front of her. She felt like time had stopped momentarily. She quietly sang to the colt and a calm peace fell over them like rain. Then the piercing cry announced the start of the race.

Chapter 17

Dirt flew in all directions as the horses sped off. Riders and spectators whooped and hollered all at once. Dusty took off so fast Spupaleena had to grab a piece of mane and center herself on his back. She grabbed hold with her knees, leaning forward and letting him have full rein. The course was marked with bits of cloth and lined with warm bodies.

Spupaleena pulled in front of most of the pack and paced herself. The evil snake took the lead. They had traveled about fifty yards before ascending a rugged, twisting mountain path. The finish mark was actually behind the racers. At the top of the mountain, they would horseshoe around and head in the direction of the Columbia River.

The horses slowed to a steady climb, picking their way through downfall and over fallen logs from the harsh winter and winds that blew off the river. The incline was steep. Some horses attempted to lunge up but were reined back to a walk. In spots, they had to S-curve though rocks and moss. Spupaleena was encouraged because there was no shale in the area. However, some of the rocks they had to cross were mighty jagged. God-willing, no horses would get cut.

Burning lungs were filled with hot air, and sweat gathered on the horses' hides. It was one hundred plus degrees outside, and even though they were in the shade of the forest, the blistering air hung thick. It was hard enough for the contestants to breathe, let alone the animals.

A few horses that were not in adequate shape should have been stopped in order to catch their breath. At this point, Dusty was a handful of horses behind the leaders. He dug in and walked a steady, rhythmic pace like a steam locomotive climbing a hill. "You're doing great," Spupaleena said in her best supportive voice. She hung on trying to lean forward and get off his back so he could climb with less weight bearing down on him.

Spupaleena glanced up and saw Hahoola<u>who</u> kicking his stallion and urging him on with unsympathetic words and a harsh tone to his voice. Everything about him irritated Spupaleena. She actually felt bad for his horse. He was a beautiful and powerful animal who deserved love and respect, not to mention a kind hand.

Hahoola<u>who</u> grabbed at the rein, pulling on his horse's mouth at each turn. She realized the creature obeyed not out of love of his owner, but a gripping fear. Spupaleena found herself saying a little prayer for the animal. She hoped to win just to give him a kinder home. The red-roan would not be bred for the color, but for his self-assured mind and kind heart.

Turning her attention back to her own matters, Spupaleena held on tight until Dusty crowned the top of the mountain. She scooted herself once again to the center of his back. She let him trot a few strides, and off they went. They cantered on the top of the ridge through checkers of grassy patches and boulders.

Peering over her shoulder, she caught site of the other horses several lengths behind. Only a few horses were in front of her. The animals lagging behind were already lathered and tired. She wondered why some of them had even entered the race. They clearly lacked the endurance for this type of event. In fact, the owners came up short of intelligence when it came to the right type training. She was sure they had no idea how to properly condition their horses—a whole bundle of fools.

Dusty was just getting warmed up. He was sweating, but due to the temperature, not for lack of fitness. They had eaten up four miles with three to go. Turning the bend, the pair headed down the draw, which was fast but not overly steep. All Spupaleena needed to do was shift her weight slightly backward, and Dusty sped up into a full gallop. "Lord, stick me to this horse," she prayed.

She tried to stay still and relaxed, sitting upright like the trees. Wrapping her feet around Dusty's barrel, she clung tight. She was thankful her doeskin leggings gripped his hair like bark on a tree. It seemed like only seconds until they hit the bottom of the mountain, which was a relief after a few tree limbs had slapped her in the face on the narrow path. Her cheeks stung, and she was sure they were scratched and bloody. But it was all a long way from her heart.

They were hustling toward a creek when she heard a yell and breaking branches behind her. She whipped her head around to see a horse and rider toppling over. The colt must have tripped over some downfall. She flipped her head forward and kept on going, saying a quick prayer for them both. She pressed her knees against the colt, trying to relax her legs and avoid cramping.

The creek approach was steep. Hahoolawho forced his stallion to jump in and Spupaleena could hear the crack of hoof on rock. He let out a piercing cry in hopes of urging his stallion on. Spupaleena, on the other hand, reined in her colt and let him pick his way through the rushing creek. A lame horse was a finished horse. She had too much at stake to have an injured mount.

The water splashed and cooled them both. How refreshing it felt. Spupaleena smiled for a brief moment then again grew serious. She focused on the upcoming turns that hugged the side of a stony cliff. They had to be careful covering the rock that littered the pathway at such a swift pace. The off-side offered a steep drop off. It was life saving to just allow the horses to have their head and pick a safe path across the trail.

While coming around a corner, one of the horses ahead of her screamed in pain. A rock bruised the frog of his foot. They slowed down as Spupaleena carefully rounded the pair and sped past. If the rider were humane at all, the race would be over for the two of them.

Hahoolawho glanced back and hollered something, but Spupaleena paid no mind; she centered her thoughts on the next leg of the race. Huge pine trees had been felled by men just for this race. She had jumped Dusty over smaller logs, but nothing of this magnitude. She caught herself holding her breath and blew it out.

Sighing, she sunk into his back and relaxed her body as much as she could without the support of a saddle. She grabbed a bigger chunk of Dusty's mane and leaned forward as he took the first jump. She slid to one side, and her head snapped back, but she managed to say aboard.

Hanging on tight, she leaned into the next jump, gliding over with a little more finesse. Each consecutive leap was easier and more balanced than the one prior, and Spupaleena gleaned more confidence with every hurdle.

Dusty picked up the pace as his hooves tore through the grass valley. She let him open up, tapping his rump a few quick times with her whip, and he passed riders until he was neck to shoulder with Quiy Sket.

Hahoolawho kicked at them, and all Spupaleena could do was laugh. The twisted look on his face spoke loudly, but she turned a deaf ear as she lifted her gaze to prepare for the upcoming log she was about to take on. Spupaleena scooted the colt over so she was no longer crowding the fool and his stud. If he was going to win, it would be honestly. Dusty effortlessly bound over the final log and pressed on.

The Columbia River was now in view. They would have to rush down a hill and cover some ground downriver before attempting to cross safely. There were a few options each rider could choose from. Spupaleena opted to navigate through some turns and downward slopes while Hahoola<u>who</u> broke off to slide down the steepest drop off possible. He seemed to enjoy earning his nickname. Only an idiot would take a horse down that steep of a grade littered with rocks and downfall.

Spupaleena could feel the colt's muscles tighten from overexertion, but his heart was nothing short of courage. He had the will of a hungry cougar hunting a deer. Her leggings were soaked, and the inside of her legs were raw. But she could not, would not, lose Smok'n Dust, not if it killed her. He had won her heart long ago, and she would fight for him, and he sensed it.

She wound down the hill and straight for the bank. Spupaleena knew if she relaxed and let Dusty feel her trust, they would clear the river. She stayed close to the bank as it led her to the crossing point. She assumed the fool was ahead, but she saw no sign of him.

Leaning her arm forward and hunkering down, Spupaleena let the colt fly. There was a breeze coming off the river, and she envisioned herself riding on its current. The crossing was in sight, and she swallowed hard, glancing back; still nothing. She wondered if he took a tumble and rolled down the incline. She hoped not for the stallion's sake.

Turning, she tried to slow the colt down, but he took hold of the bit and slammed into the river. His head went under water and then shot back up, he snorted and lunged forward. Spupaleena went under and came up choking, managing to hang on tightly. The river floor plunged down a few feet, causing Dusty to leap a handful of steps before he was able to swim ahead.

Spupaleena struggled to keep her legs at Dusty's sides, so she let them float behind, gripping his mane. Her knuckles grew white as she clung tight. The current was strong enough to carry them down river in no time. Her legs burned with the heaviness of the wet buckskin that anchored her behind, but the cold river soon numbed them, masking the pain. Her fingers ached and her forearms began to cramp.

Dusty leaned his head forward and paddled with his legs. They were soon on the other side. He scurried up the bank and rounded his back forcing his hindquarters to thrust ahead. Spupaleena was so exhausted she almost lost her hold. Dusty was just as tired.

A splash and cry echoed off the rushing water as Hahoolawho and Quiy Sket plunged into the river. Spupaleena was flabbergasted, realizing she was in the lead. Dusty assembled every last ounce of will and unexpectedly sped up.

Spupaleena saw the two men holding the finish rope. There was a third figure standing in the shadows that puzzled her. As she advanced toward the men, she saw that it was her father. She gasped. He stood to the side, behind them on the bank of the hill. He was yelling and waving his arms, motioning her to the end. She reached back and gave Dusty a few extra taps on the rump, and she felt like his hooves were floating on top of the earth below. His breaths were hard and fast, and his eyes were glued on the finish rope.

Carmen Peone

Dusty burned up the ground beneath him as tears streamed down Spupaleena's face. She crouched low, with her arms as forward as they could reach. She tucked her chin to her chest, giving the colt all the room he needed to let loose and run. No other rider came close. She crossed the finish rope. The men's hands that held the rope burned from the force of it being ripped away. Skumhist jumped up and down like a little child and tossed his hat into the air. Spupaleena sat up, looking ahead and just let Dusty gallop on freely.

"Thank you, Lord!" was all she could declare as she choked on her emotions. Tears streamed down her face as she looked to the heavens, smiling as the sun shone on her face.

She rode for God and God alone.

Arrow Lakes Word Index

Note: <u>K</u> sound like regular *k*, but in the back of the throat, a guttural sound.

Chapter One:

Word   *Meaning*
Pronunciation/Sounds Like

Hahoola<u>who</u> *Rattlesnake*
Ha (hah)- hoola- <u>who</u> (soft blowing sound)

Spupaleena *Rabbit*
Spup- a- leena (like Tina)

Quiy S<u>k</u>et *Black Rain*
Qu- iy (eye)- S<u>k</u>et (like jet, the <u>*k*</u> - back of throat)

Kewa   *Yes*
  Ke (key)- wa (wah)

Lim Lumt   *Thank You*
  Lim (rhymes with Tim)- lumt

Skumhist   *Black Bear*
  Skum (scum)- hist (rhymes with beast)

Mistum   *Father*
  Mist- um

Lthkickha   *Older Sister*
  Lth (see sound guide)- kick- ha (rhymes with ma)

Pekam   *Bobcat*
  Pe (sounds like Pea)- kam (rhymes with Sam)

Sintahoos   *Brother*
  Sin- ta (taw)- hoos (rhymes with loose)

Hamis-hamis   *Morning Dove*
  Ha (haw)- mis (miss) repeat

Sneena   *Owl*
  Snee- na (nuh)

Soo ya pee   *White Man*
  Soo (rhymes with Sue)- ya (yaw)- pee (pea)

It Huh pa pa Latsa   *Sleeping Moose*
  It- <u>huh</u> (blow in back of throat)- pa (paw) –pa (paw)-
Latsa (sounds like lots-a)

Chapter Two

Word   *Meaning*
  Pronunciation/Sounds Like

Stimteema   *Maternal Grandmother*
  S-tim-tee (tea)- ma (muh) (Also Tima) tim-a

Loot   *No*
  Loo (Lou)- t

Wi   *Yes*
  Like why but the "y" is cut short

Simill<u>k</u>ameen   *Swan*
  Si-mill<u>k</u>-a-meen (sounds like mean)

Qual<u>k</u>hun   *Porcupine*
  Qual (sounds like Quail- <u>k</u>(gutteral)- hun (sounds
like hon)

Ohuh teelut   *Baby*
  O (oh)- <u>huh</u> (blow in back of throat)- tee (tea)-
lut(rhymes with put)

Chapter Three

Word   *Meaning*
  Pronunciation/Sounds Like

Stumpkeelt   *Daughter*
  Stump- k (back of throat)- eelt

Hast Eelth Qua Quaost, mistum   *Good morning, father*
  Has-t Ee-lth (see sound guide) - Qua-Quost (rhymes with host)- mist-um

Kukneeya   *Listen*
  K (back of throat)- u (as in m*u*d)- k (back of throat) nee (like knee)- ya (yaw)

Nee Ap Kukneeya   *Forever Listening*
  Nee (like Knee)- Ap (like n*ap*)- Kukneeya (above)

Pelpalwheechula   *Butterfly*
  Pel (rhymes with bell)- pal- wheech (rhymes with beach)- u (you)- la (luh)

Kawup   *Horse*
  K- a (u)- wup

Chapter Four

Word   *Meaning*
Pronunciation/Sounds Like

Sweenompt   *Handsome*
Swee- no (new)- mpt

Chapter Seven

Word   *Meaning*
Pronunciation/Sounds Like

In hamink anwee   *I love you*
In- ha (haw)- mink- an (on)- wee

Chapter Ten

Word   *Meaning*
Pronunciation/Sounds Like

K̲ook̲yuma   *Small/Tiny*
K̲ (back of throat)- oo- k̲-yuma (you)- ma (mah)

Oh̲uh̲ teelut (see chapter two)

Chapter Thirteen

Word   *Meaning*
  Pronunciation/Sounds Like

Taka Takum   *Thunder*
  Tak (talk)- a- ta (tuh)- kum (come)

American words:

Tule is pronounced Two- lee (Stem of the Cattail)

Zeri is pronounced Zeree- In the Old Testaments of the Bible.